ABIOGENESIS

NCP

Be sure to check out our website for the very best in fiction at fantastic prices!

When you visit our webpage, you can:

* Read excerpts of currently available books
* View cover art of upcoming books and current releases
* Find out more about the talented artists who capture the magic of the writer's imagination on the covers
* Order books from our backlist
* Find out the latest NCP and author news--including any upcoming book signings by your favorite NCP author
* Read author bios and reviews of our books
* Get NCP submission guidelines
* And so much more!

We offer a 20% discount on all new ebook releases!
(Sorry, but short stories are not included in this offer.)

We also have contests and sales regularly, so be sure to visit our webpage to find the best deals in ebooks and paperbacks! To find out about our new releases as soon as they are available, please be sure to sign up for our newsletter (http://www.newconceptspublishing.com/newsletter.htm) or join our reader group (http://groups.yahoo.com/group/new_concepts_pub/join) !

The newsletter is available by double opt in only and our customer information is *never* shared!

Visit our webpage at:
www.newconceptspublishing.com

Abiogenesis is an original publication of NCP. This work has never before appeared in book form. This work is a novel. Any similarity to actual persons or events is purely coincidental.

New Concepts Publishing
5202 Humphreys Rd.
Lake Park, GA 31636

ISBN 1-58608-702-9

NCP books are available at special quantity discounts for bulk purchases for sales promotions, premiums, fund raising, or educational use. For details, write, email, or phone New Concepts Publishing, 5202Humphreys Rd., Lake Park, GA 31636, ncp@newconceptspublishing.com, Ph. 229-257-0367, Fax 229-219-1097.

First NCP Paperback Printing: 2005

Printed in the United States of America

Other books available by Kaitlyn O'Connor from
NCP:

The Claiming
The Lion's Woman
Below
Guardian of the Storm
When Night Falls
Exiled
Cyborg

ABIOGENESIS

Kaitlyn O'Connor

Futuristic Romance

New Concepts   Georgia

Chapter One

Dalia VH570 stared at the bright, white light above her, watching it flicker as she felt her thoughts dissolve into the same nothingness as the whiteness that surrounded her. She had always hated physical examinations. She just wasn't certain why.

The prick of something sharp jolted Dalia into sudden, crystal clear alertness and the absolute certainty of danger. Opening her eyes, she surveyed her surroundings, searching for the threat she sensed.

She was still in the examination room, but she was bound to the table now. Turning her head, she looked at the man who'd just stabbed a syringe into her arm.

Her movement brought his gaze to hers, and she saw his eyes dilate instantly with fear, guilt, and the certainty that he was looking into the face of death. His reaction forced a healthy shot of adrenaline through her body and her heart leapt into overtime, pumping it through her. Gritting her teeth, she concentrated, tensing every muscle and sinew in her body, and heaved upward, breaking the restraints. The technician was still staring at her stupidly when she gripped his hand. Snatching the syringe from her arm, she drove it into his carotid artery, depressing the plunger.

His eyes rolled back into his head. The saliva in his mouth boiled, foaming, spilling between his gasping lips. She sat up, grasping his throat, half lifting him from the floor. "You tried to kill me. Why?"

His mouth worked. He gagged, coughed up spittle and blood. "Help me," he pleaded.

Dalia shook him. "First tell me why."

"Gestating... you're gestating. Never supposed to be able...."

She stared at him blankly, trying to understand the word, trying to figure out what it had to do with his attempt to kill her. "What is this word?"

"Reproduction. To bear young," he gasped, clawing at her hand frantically.

She dropped him, staring down at him as he sprawled on the floor beside the gurney she sat on. Tossing the sterile sheet off that had covered her, she slipped to the floor. "A child? A baby? You tried to kill me because I'm ... breeding? It's only a fifty thousand credit fine!"

He shook his head frantically. "Not human. Not human."

She stared at him uncomprehendingly for several moments but finally lifted her head, realizing at last that the alert was sounding, had been since she'd broken her restraints. She blinked, calculating the time. Anywhere from three to five minutes had passed. The exits would be blocked by now and guarded. A contingent of guards would be racing toward this room.

She glanced down at the technician, but he'd stopped gurgling. His eyes were wide and staring now.

A wave of nausea washed over her. That should have been her. It would have been if she hadn't awakened when he'd speared her with the needle. She'd never killed another human being before, though, and she couldn't decide whether she was more horrified at having a hand in his death, revolted by what a human being looked like in their death throes, or because she'd been a hair's breadth from experiencing rather than witnessing. She didn't have time to analyze her distress, however. Shelving it for the moment, she glanced around the examination room, but no windows magically appeared. There was still only the one door.

She checked the walls, the floor, the ceiling.

Why had she allowed them to take her into a room with only one exit? Her training had taught her better. It was stupid to have relaxed her guard only because the med lab belonged to the company, the company she killed for.

She'd never trusted the damned company.

Leaping up onto the examination table, she reached up toward the ceiling and realized she was still too short. She could just touch the tiles above her with her fingertips. She went up on her tiptoes, bounced. Finally, she managed to dislodge the panel above her. It was a suspended ceiling, she saw, held aloft by thin wires. She seriously doubted it would hold her weight, but she was out of options.

Leaping up again, she caught the frame that had held the tile. As she'd more than half expected, it buckled, bringing down a rain of tiles around her.

The sound of running feet, many feet, came to her. It must be a full squad.

Good, she decided. The noise they were making would help to cover the noise she made. Leaping down from the examination table, she raced across the room, bent her knees and leapt upward, her arms extended. She crashed through the tile. It hit the floor around her. The wall, she saw went all the way up, approximately ten feet. Metal girders supported the floor above her.

It was the girders or nothing.

Whirling, she raced back toward the examination table, hit it flat footed and leapt upward, catching the bottom of a girder. With an effort, she pulled herself up, but she saw the space was too small for her to walk her way across hanging by her hands. Supporting most of her weight from her arms, she pulled her legs up and swung until she could hook her heels along the girder, as well.

It was dark above the ceiling, particularly since she had only just come from a room blindingly white, but she had excellent night vision. She focused her eyes and looked around. As far as she could see, there was nothing but girders, pipe, electrical wires and ductwork. The ductwork was too small to crawl through, and too light to support her weight.

She closed her eyes, mentally tracing her path through the building and into the examination room. Only a corridor separated her from the closest outer wall of the building, but the guards were racing down that path. She took the opposite direction. It was a good deal further from the outer wall, but it was also less likely that guards would be stationed there.

Moving swiftly now, she crawled, spider like beneath the beam until she'd reached the wall she'd seen on the other side. She turned then, following it until she found an opening. A catwalk ran through it and she dropped down onto it. Looking in first one direction and then the other, she finally decided to continue as she'd begun and crawled through the opening. She'd only just cleared it when she heard the guards pounding on the examination room door. Crouching low, she ran as fast as she could.

It wouldn't take them long to figure out she was in the overhead ceiling and probably not much more than that to realize that the only way she could traverse it was along the catwalk.

She heard them behind her before she reached the outer wall.

Dropping to her stomach, she reached for the closest ceiling tile and lifted it up just enough to study the room beneath her.

It was occupied. A woman was lying on an examination table, just as Dalia had been only minutes before.

She didn't have time to be picky.

Rolling off the catwalk, she dropped through the ceiling, landing in a half crouch on the floor. Startled, the woman sat up, opening her mouth to scream. Dalia leapt at her, covering the woman's mouth with one hand and pinching the woman's carotid artery with the other. The moment the woman's eyes rolled back in her head, Dalia released her and looked around, absently checking the woman's pulse to make certain she hadn't killed her.

This room had both a window and a door. She moved to the window first, pulled the window covering aside and looked out. She was on the sixtieth floor, about half way up the building, more or less. The outside of the building was as smooth as glass. Windows broke the monotony every ten feet or so, but most likely every one was fixed just as this one was and could not be opened and were probably nearly as impossible to break.

She couldn't fly, so that was out.

There was no point in trying to go down. They would be waiting for her. Up would only work if there were crafts on the roof.

It was a med lad. There were probably a half a dozen or more on the roof at any time.

There was one slight problem.

She didn't have a stitch of clothing on and that was bound to draw attention. Shrugging, she helped herself to the tunic and trousers the woman had been wearing. They were too big, but it wouldn't be nearly as noticeable as being naked. The woman's shoes were too big, too. It was too risky to wear them, she decided. They would slow her down at the very least. At worst, the shoes could trip her if she needed to run. She slipped the stockings on to cover her bare feet and make them less noticeable, then moved to the door, opening it a crack.

No one seemed terribly excited. She saw a couple of techs strolling along one end of the corridor, notepads in hand. There was a knot of them at one end of the corridor, waiting, she realized, for an elevator or having just gotten off one.

Obviously, security still thought they had the 'danger' contained on the other side of the firewall that ran down the building.

Stepping from the room, she walked casually toward the row of elevators and punched the button that would summon one going up. As she stood waiting, several more people joined her, staring up at the display panel above the doors. Turning her head just enough she could examine each of them in her peripheral vision, she relaxed fractionally. There was no sign of security guards ... yet.

Impatience began to gnaw at her. She'd just decided to find the stairs and take them up several flights when the bells on three of the elevators dinged, announcing the arrival of the cubicles. Having already turned away and taken a step down the corridor toward the sign marked 'exit', she glanced inside the elevator she'd been standing in front of as the doors slowly began to open.

It was packed with guards ...and the one in front was holding a tracker. He glanced up as she strode away, his eyes locking on her for about two seconds. Shoving anyone aside who lay in her path, she broke into a run as she heard the guards launch themselves against the opening doors, trying to squeeze through all at once and succeeding only in bottlenecking the exit.

The doors on the fourth elevator had already begun to close as she reached it. She leapt through the rapidly narrowing opening. The timing was perfect. She'd barely landed inside when the doors slammed closed. Her last view of the corridor, however, had been of the guards charging the elevator.

They'd spotted her. They would reroute it, she knew.

Ignoring the gasps and protests of the four people already in the elevator when she'd jumped in, she moved to the control panel, studied it a moment and finally speared her fingers through the holes drilled for the buttons, grasped the panel firmly and pulled it out of the wall, exposing the circuits. Almost simultaneously, the elevator lights blinked and the cubicle ground to a halt.

They'd already tied in.

Glancing over the circuits, she saw immediately that there was no way to rewire it. She grasped the panel and wrenched it out, tossing it to one side and evoking a round of screams from the women in the group. Grasping the main feed, she pulled on the wire until she had enough to reach, then stripped the insulation from the end, felt behind her head until she found the jack and plugged directly into the computer.

It took thirty seconds to override their override, and another five to lock them out. As the elevator jolted into motion again, Dalia examined the database and found that there were four crafts on the roof, fueled and prepped to go. One of the elevators was already on the roof. The other two were on the ground level and the tenth floor.

She was about to log out when it occurred to her that now was her opportunity to discover what the computer knew about her situation. The CPU inside her brain began displaying images before her eyes almost instantly.

Gestation was an archaic form of reproduction that had been practiced by the human race until the last century. The fertilized ovum attached itself inside the female's body, within a cavity known as the womb, and lived off of the female's body until it reached a state of maturity that would allow it to survive on its own.

Dalia frowned. *How is the parasite introduced into the host to begin with?*

Male and female each carried an element, the female an egg or ovum, which contained the DNA of the female host. The male donor provided sperm, which contained the male's DNA and would activate the egg and set off a chain reaction. The male would deliver his DNA via sexual intercourse.

Dalia mulled that over for a moment. She hadn't engaged in sex, at all. It was prohibited by the company to anyone in her position, an infraction punishable by termination. She'd always assumed they meant termination of employment, however. *In the event that the female did not have sexual intercourse with a male, was there another method of delivery? Or was it possible for the female to manipulate the ovum herself and induce it to begin to replicate cells?*

This method of reproduction was imprecise. Often the female would become impregnated when reproduction was infeasible or undesirable due to economic, health or social conditions. Occasionally, the male or female who wished to reproduce would be found to be infertile. If the male was infertile, and unable to provide his DNA, a donor would be found who was a desirable substitute and his DNA would be introduced into the female via medical procedure.

It still didn't make any sense to her. They'd impregnated her and now had decided to terminate both her and the pregnancy? She shook it off. She didn't have time to study it now. *Status?*

Passing the 100th floor.

Locate the guards for me.

Ten in elevator number one, passing the 15th floor. Five in elevator number three, passing the 40th floor. Five on elevator number two, egressing onto the roof now. Thirty on the ground floor level.

Chapter Two

Dalia removed the jack and turned to study the other passengers. They were huddled into one corner, staring at her as if she was some sort of monster. She supposed she could see their point, but it irritated the hell out of her anyway.

She had maybe five minutes before they reached the roof. That meant they had five minutes to deploy and be waiting for her. She could stop the elevator and take the stairs, but she wasn't certain that would give her any advantage. Even though she'd locked them out of the computer system, they would probably be expecting the possibility and have that exit covered too.

There was no cover for them on the roof beyond the craft moored there, but then they must know she was unarmed. There wasn't any reason for them to take cover except as a precaution in case she'd somehow located a weapon.

She finally decided they would probably assume assault positions anyway. The only thing you could count on about militia was that they always went by the book, and they always followed orders. Obviously, they didn't want or need to take her alive. They wanted her dead. That meant they would be stationed and ready to catch her in a crossfire.

She glanced at the other passengers speculatively, but she knew they were as expendable as she was. The objective wasn't to slaughter them, but the security guards weren't likely to quibble about having to go through them to get her, so using them as a shield was out.

Besides, she didn't want to be responsible for their deaths.

"They're waiting for me on the roof. If you don't want to die today, lie down on the floor as flat as you can and clasp your hands on top of your heads. With any luck, the fire will miss you." They gaped at her uncomprehendingly for several moments, then scrambled to comply, fighting briefly over who would have the position closest to the door. As she felt the elevator decelerating, Dalia jumped up onto the handrail that ran around the cubicle, bracing her hands above her head to balance herself.

The moment the door began to open, laser fire pelted the interior of the cubicle, covering almost every square inch of the walls from about one foot up to the ceiling. The side of the elevator protected Dalia as she'd hoped it would. She held her breath, waiting until she heard some call a cease fire, allowing the seconds to tick off as she envisioned them slowly stepping from their cover, advancing far enough to look into the elevator to see if they'd gotten her.

The bodies on the floor would confuse them, hopefully, for critical moments.

The trick was to time it precisely, move before they realized she wasn't one of the bodies lying on the floor of the elevator.

She held her breath, focusing on listening and interpreting the sounds she heard since she couldn't see; cautious, carefully placed footsteps--three pair. Two were still under cover.

Abruptly, she swung into action, landing on the floor of the elevator and bursting through the doors as they began to close once more. As she'd hoped, she caught them completely off guard. The three closest to the elevator opened their eyes and mouths wide in surprise. She hit the first one full tilt, bowling him over. She clotheslined the second with an extended arm, grabbing his weapon from his slackened grip even as he executed a flip. The third man, she took out with the butt of the weapon she'd grabbed. She whirled in a circle then, laying out random fire and catching the remaining two guards even as they finally managed to begin firing on her.

Within moments, five dead or groaning men lay on the flight deck. Gasping for breath, she surveyed them, her hands on her hips. "Never send a man to do a cyborg's job," she muttered in satisfaction, but then mentally shrugged. She was a rogue hunter, trained and biotechnologically enhanced to bring down rogue cyborgs, and she would've still had her hands full if they had sent even two. It was fortunate for her that they'd made an error in judgment and sent men instead.

She frowned. They either hadn't anticipated having any problem terminating her--which seemed unlikely given her training, or the decision to terminate her was of short standing.

Shaking off her questions and the weariness and apathy in the aftermath of battle, Dalia moved over them, quickly collecting their weapons and then headed for the nearest craft. Tossing the weapons into the patient bay of the ambulance craft, she scrambled into the cockpit, examined the layout to identify the craft and began flipping switches to activate the engines. Even as the craft began to lift off, the doors of one of the other elevators opened and men began to pour out, firing at her.

She punched the craft into hyper acceleration and it shot upwards and away in a sharp slingshot like motion--not, unfortunately, before it caught a dozen hits. The craft almost immediately became unstable and she knew they'd managed to hit something critical. Struggling to keep it level, she allowed it to drop toward the upper level traffic airway forty floors below her.

Bright dots lit up her radar screen both above and below her, looking like a swarm of insects. She glanced up through the viewing bubble and counted two crafts descending fast. They were ambulances like the one she'd taken, and the craft itself had no firepower. As long as she didn't let them get close enough to catch her in the sights of their handheld weapons, the risk of taking another hit was slim.

She wasn't certain if the craft needed another hit to bring it down, however. It began bucking and jolting as she hit the airway. The computer failed to adjust to oncoming traffic and she slammed into the protective force field of another craft, bounced off of it and ping ponged against three more before she dropped beneath the airway in a forward gliding descent.

In truth, it wasn't much of a glide. The craft continued to bounce and drop erratically in a controlled crash, as if it were striking solid objects instead of air currents. She managed to drop through the mid-level airway without incident, mostly because the heavy traffic was on the third level she'd already passed. A layer of greenish-yellow smog lay below her, obscuring her view of the lower airway. She landed on the roof of a passing craft when she reached the lowest level, was repelled by the protective field that surrounded it and nose dived through the airway, free falling for some twenty feet before she managed to kick the ambulance craft in the ass and get it going again.

Androids, cyborgs and pedestrians thronged the walks below her. When they looked up and saw her craft falling toward them, they scattered like fall leaves caught in a strong cross wind--in every direction. Despite that, she managed to set the craft down on the walk without smearing anyone. It's forward momentum responded sluggishly to her attempts to brake, however, and the craft slid along the walk for nearly a hundred yards before coming to rest against the base of one of the buildings that surrounded the walks like mountains, blocking so much of the light that the ground level lay in perpetual night except for artificial lighting.

The moment the craft finally stopped, Dalia threw off her restraints and struggled to stand. As far as she could tell she had suffered no more than bruises and a few minor cuts, but she knew adrenaline was pushing her now. She could be hurt much worse and not know it right away.

Regardless, she had to put as much distance between herself and the craft as possible before the guards caught up with her. Sorting through the weapons, she grabbed the two that had the fullest charges, slung one on each shoulder and scrambled out of the craft. Gawkers had already begun to converge on the downed craft when she emerged. Ignoring them, she strode purposefully toward the group milling about and pushed through. They parted before her, as if they feared she might be contaminated with something.

When she'd cleared the crowd, she broke into a jog and finally a run, glancing to her left and right each time she passed a narrow alley in search of one that was unoccupied. She'd begun to despair that there was even so much as a square inch of ground level space not inhabited when she raced past a vacant throughway. Stopping abruptly, she reversed directions and raced down it till she came to the first intersection. She began to weave her way back and forth through the narrow alleys until she came at last to the slum area of the city.

It, too, was occupied, but by the denizens of the dark--the 'subhuman' culture the upstanding citizens of the city were prone to consider did not exist. Unless the company was offering a reward for her, it was unlikely anyone would be interested enough in her to give the guards searching for her any tips.

Of course, they wouldn't need any information if she couldn't get rid of the locator surgically implanted in her hip, but she couldn't get rid of it until she could shake her pursuit long enough to stop.

Added to that little problem was the fact that she'd had to leave without her uniform--which held a med kit.

Tired now, she slowed to a brisk walk, stopping each time she found a derelict sprawled drunkenly on the walk and checking him for a knife. She found a razor on the second man she checked and studied it doubtfully. It was rusted, and she wasn't certain it could cut deeply enough, but beggars couldn't be choosers.

Straightening, she looked around for a lighted area and moved toward it. She didn't like the idea of standing in the light, but she didn't want to butcher her hip either. She needed the light to see what she was doing. After scanning the immediate area for threat and deciding it was minimal, she set her weapons down, shucked the trousers and probed the flesh of her hip until she found the locator.

Without giving herself time to think it over, she sliced the flesh as deeply as the razor would cut. Seconds passed before the pain caught up with her brain. She'd already dug her fingers into the cut, grasped the locator and yanked it free of the bone before fire poured through her. Gasping at the wave of dizziness that washed over her, she dropped the locator to the pavement, picked up one of the weapons and smashed it with the butt.

Blood was gushing from the cut. She studied it for several moments, but she knew there were no major veins in that area. Regardless, she couldn't allow it to continue to bleed. They'd be able to follow the blood trail almost as easily as the locator. Then, too, she might run out of fluids before she managed to get hold of a medical kit.

She didn't like it, but she didn't have any options. Lifting the weapon, she set it on its lowest setting and carefully sited it along the cut, firing off one quick burst.

The pain didn't take nearly as much time to reach her brain that time. She staggered back and fell to her knees, fighting the blackness that threatened to overwhelm her.

Dimly, she saw she'd attracted some attention from the local lowlifes. Lifting the weapon with an effort, she fired off several warning shots. When they scattered, she grabbed her trousers and the other weapon and began moving again. She wanted nothing so much as to crash somewhere, if only for fifteen or twenty minutes, but she couldn't afford the luxury until she'd put a lot of distance between herself and the locator she'd just destroyed. Her pursuit would almost certainly have triangulated on that position by now.

The faintness didn't recede. She had to fight it every step of the way. Finally, she managed to put at least a mile between her and the locator, before she reached a point where she knew she couldn't go another step without falling on her face.

Pausing, she leaned back against the wall of a building and searched the area. She hadn't seen anyone in a while, but that didn't mean they weren't there, watching, waiting for her to let her guard down so that they could steal anything she had of value and probably kill her in the process.

The building she was leaning against was ancient, deserted, crumbling. She climbed through the nearest opening and studied it, moving slowly through, her weapon at the ready. Skittering noises filtered to her from time to time, but she thought it must be some sort of animals. They didn't make enough noise to be human.

She came upon a partial stair leading upward and debated briefly whether it would be better to find a hiding place on one of the other floors or on the ground floor. Finally, she decided to try the second floor. It would give her a little lead time if she heard anyone coming. She could, if she had to, jump from the second floor without doing too much damage to herself ... as long as she was careful to land correctly.

Shouldering her weapon, she placed her back against the wall and moved carefully from step to step until she reached a gap. Checking the strength of the handrail to see if it would support her if the stair collapsed, she leapt the distance, coming down on her wounded hip. Her knee buckled, but she managed to catch herself with the railing.

When she'd reached the top, she turned to study the stairs and finally pulled one of the weapons from her shoulder and cut a larger section out. It would be far easier, she knew, for her to leap the hole downward than for anyone to leap it coming up. She found another set of stairs near the rear of the building, or rather a stairwell. Those stairs were completely gone.

The place reeked of death. As tempted as she was to just find a corner and collapse, she knew she couldn't rest until she'd assured herself she had the place to herself. The building had looked like it had at least six floors, even as ancient as it was, but there were only two floors accessible from the floor she was on. The upper floors had begun to slowly collapse down upon each other.

She found a badly decomposed body two floors up, which explained the god-awful smell and the lack of other occupants.

Relieved, she made her way down again, found a comfortable corner that was relatively free of debris, and collapsed. She'd hardly even settled when blackness closed in around her. She was disoriented for several moments when she woke. Sluggishly, her mind kicked in and memory flooded back to her. She had no idea how long she'd slept--there wasn't enough sunlight filtering so far beneath the city to judge from the sun's movement. She could've been out mere minutes, or hours, or even days--but she struggled to her feet and checked her perimeter.

Satisfied that they hadn't discovered her and surrounded the building while she rested, she found a corner to relieve herself and then returned to her corner and sat down to figure out what options she might have.

There weren't a lot. She didn't know why they wanted her dead, but they seemed pretty damned set on seeing it done.

The tech had seemed to indicate that it was because she was gestating, but that was nearly as inconceivable as the fact that she was gestating at all. No one *bore* young anymore. It was too unpredictable and too inconvenient. If they happened to want one, they bought a permit and ordered one from the med lab. They hadn't practiced the 'natural' way of doing it in nearly a century. As far as she knew, though, there was no law against it, certainly not a death sentence, anyway.

She wouldn't have been surprised if they'd arrested her for breeding without a permit. She would've expected something like that, if she'd been engaging in sexual activity and stupid enough to do it without protection. But that would've been followed by a brief trial, maybe, and then release as soon as she coughed up the fine and bought a permit.

Maybe it was a law that was still on the books, but hadn't been used in so long that nobody, except the lawmakers and the law enforcers, even knew it was there anymore?

It seemed possible. The morons never got rid of laws. They just made more when the need arose. There were laws still on the books, she knew, from centuries before, laws that people didn't even understand anymore because nothing they pertained to even existed now.

Briefly, she wondered if there was any way to remove the parasite, but it occurred to her fairly quickly that that wasn't going to help. If there'd been a way, or if that would've made a difference, they would have done that instead of deciding to kill her. She hadn't come cheap. The company had spent a lot of money training her to be a rogue hunter, and even more bioengineering her for strength, stamina, high pain tolerance, computer assisted mental capabilities, and a broader hearing and sight range.

Anyway, she felt strangely possessive about it. She didn't know why, and she didn't really want to examine it at the moment. But she did know she didn't want to make any kind of decision about, possibly, removing it until she'd had time to think it through and consider every possibility.

Besides, the tech had been dying. How much faith could she place in anything he'd told her? The company's reasons for trying to terminate her could be something else entirely.

Unfortunately, no amount of carefully reconstructing her actions over the past month, or the month before that, produced any possibilities. She hadn't failed her last mission and, even if she had, punishment for failure was only a death sentence if the rogue dealt it out. The company was content to fine her all her pay and half her previous paycheck.

Shaking her head, Dalia finally decided she couldn't waste time trying to figure it out. It was enough to know she was dead if ... when they caught her. The only chance that she could see of turning the 'when' to 'if' was if she managed to get off world. Sooner or later, if she stayed, they were going to catch her, with or without the locator.

She could die a slow death here without food or water, or risk getting caught going for supplies. One retina scan and she was done for. Besides, she wouldn't be able to buy anything without having her barcode scanned, even in the black market, and once they had that, they'd have a bead on her location.

They would be expecting her to try to get off planet, though.

Her only chance, as far as she could see, was to locate a smuggler and either take the ship, or bargain a ride, and that meant she was going to have to figure out a way out of the dome.

Chapter Three

It took her almost a week to locate a man who claimed he not only knew a way out of the dome undetected, but also knew where the smugglers usually landed. It stood to reason that he would since there wouldn't be any other reason for leaving the protection of the dome.

The problem was, Dalia had nothing to bargain with. She finally convinced him to take her, however, by telling him if he did she wouldn't blow his head off. He wasn't terribly thrilled with the bargain, but he led her through the tunnels that eventually carried them beyond the city without detection.

By that time she had no problem blending with the natives. She'd had very little to eat, very little sleep, no access to bathing facilities and, since the clothes she was standing in were all she had, she looked as ragged and unkempt as everyone else. She didn't like it, but she was inclined to see it as an advantage.

The quality of the air inside the dome wasn't that great in the lower regions, but the air beyond the dome was the next thing to unbreathable. She still had her weapons, but the lack of a mask put her at a distinct disadvantage when the smugglers had more manpower and firepower at their disposal than she did.

The moment they reached the landing area, she saw immediately that simply blending wasn't going to be enough. There was no way she was going to get close enough to either overpower the smugglers and steal a ship, or slip on board. Releasing her 'guide', she watched until she was certain he was headed back the way they'd come and wouldn't alert the smugglers, and then settled down to study them and watch for an opportunity.

She'd been fully aware that smuggling was rife, but she hadn't realized that trafficking in stolen and/or illegal merchandise was done on quite as grand a scale as this. When she arrived, a large ship was already at the rendezvous point. More than a dozen smugglers had piled off of it. A third were busy unloading, a third loading new merchandise and the rest pacing restlessly about the activities with some fairly intimidating firepower.

Before they had even completed their business, a second craft nearly as large set down at a little distance and proceeded pretty much as the first had, off loading on one side and on loading on the other.

With decent air, or a mask, she might have been able to take four or five men. She wasn't stupid enough, or desperate enough to consider taking on crews as large as this, particularly when she was fairly certain that it would take no more than a hint of threat for them to combine forces.

She had very little food, however, and not a great deal of time. After a little while, she decided to change positions and see if another position would provide her with a better opportunity.

To her surprise, it did, but it had nothing to do with either of the two large ships she'd been watching. As she made her way around the perimeter, a relatively small, very sleek, racer settled into the rubble-strewn field at a little distance from the other two ships.

This might be doable.

The craft was designed for short, very fast hops, from planet to planet--and required no more than a pilot as crew or perhaps a pilot and copilot. There was no way it was being employed to haul cargo. It was too small to carry much and too short-range to go far--unless the pilot was insane enough to use the wormholes--which, upon reflection, she supposed he must.

If the pilot was smuggling anything, it was human cargo-- escaped slaves or criminals fleeing justice--or possibly rogue cyborgs. He would want privacy to load his cargo. The fact that he'd landed so far from the other two ships seemed to bear up her theory.

She settled down to wait. It wasn't until the first of the two larger ships had lifted off that the gangplank was finally let down. Minutes passed. Finally, a man appeared at the top of the gangplank, stood looking out for several moments, and finally sauntered almost casually down the gangplank and stepped off of it.

The only weapons he had on him were strapped to his waist, a pistol holstered on one side and a three-foot blade on the other.

She stared at the blade. It indicated a strong familiarity with some primitive culture somewhere in the universe, but she couldn't see it well enough from this distance to place it. Not that it mattered. In the first place, she didn't particularly care where she went so long as she could elude the company for long enough to figure out what was going on and how it had come about that she'd suddenly become high on their list of public enemies. In the second, it supported the theory of rogues.

In general, cyborgs were at least half human, or half biological materials anyway, and all of that on the exterior, but anyone familiar with cyborgs could spot them within minutes. The were just ... not quite human, regardless of their appearance. It was often hard to put your finger on just what it was, but there was always something that gave them away, even to people not particularly looking or not particularly interested. The only way they could truly disappear was to find a culture too primitive to know what a cyborg was.

The question was, was he doing it for the money? For the adventure? Or because he was one of those fanatical assholes always trying to change the universe?

The latter made her want to puke. She despised fanatics, whatever their particular brand of insanity was, because they were not only incredibly boring and annoying, but they were also dangerous. They, almost inevitably, managed to convince huge numbers of 'followers' to believe them and usually managed to get them killed.

At this particular moment, however, it could prove useful.

Money was a problem. She had plenty of credits saved up, but she wasn't certain it was enough to tempt a smuggler of this caliber. If it wasn't, and he scanned her barcode for the money, she would be located in short order.

Finally, she decided to move a little closer and get a better look at him.

She managed to get several yards closer before she ran out of cover. She discovered it didn't particularly help her, however. Naturally enough, it was dark. Smugglers didn't land in the daylight, and it was smoggy as bedamned, as well. The poor visibility wasn't as much a problem, however, as the fact that her feminine side took that inopportune moment to kick in and completely distracted her.

He was, quite possibly, the finest specimen of a male she'd ever set eyes on. Even her male counterparts weren't generally so beautifully enhanced. Her first good look at him impacted on her as physically as if she'd been hit by a grenade concussion. She felt as if she'd been body slammed, too stunned to think for several moments. Finally, her training kicked in and she settled behind the pile of rubble and frowned, wondering what had just happened.

Not only was she certain she'd never had a reaction like that to a male before, she couldn't even remember experiencing anything even close. Her training had been thorough and nothing had been left to chance, certainly not something as predictable and inevitable as sexual attraction. Very little ever managed to break through her conditioning as a soldier and throw her off kilter. Some sort of chemical imbalance related to the gestation, she wondered?

The sounds of the second craft lifting off jogged her from her abstraction and into action.

She peered at the pilot, saw that he'd been distracted, as well, and began to move quickly around the ship while he stood watching the ship's ascent. Coming upon him from behind, she placed the barrel of her weapon against the center of his back, directly over his heart. "I need passage off of this rock, and I don't particularly care who I have to kill to get it. Take me, and I'll pay you for your trouble and you can get on with your life. Give me any trouble and I'll kill you."

The moment the barrel of her weapon dug into his back, he went perfectly still. As she finished her little speech, however, he moved, so fast her jaw didn't have time to drop in surprise, snatching her weapon from her hands so hard and fast she was surprised he didn't take her fingers with it.

"I only take rogues," he said coolly, taking the weapon in both hands and bending it into a bow, as if it had been made of putty instead of titanium alloy.

Dalia glanced from the bent weapon into the face that had launched a million flyers. It was Reuel CO469, the first of his kind, the first cyborg rogue, the leader of all who'd come after him, and the only rogue nobody had even come close to catching in all the time she'd worked for the company.

"Oh fuck!"

A smile curled that devastating mouth. Stepping toward her, he grasped her arms, thrusting them behind her back and bringing her up hard against his massive chest. "We could. On the other hand I'm waiting for someone and I really don't like being interrupted when I'm pleasuring a beautiful woman."

"That wasn't an invitation," Dalia snapped.

His dark brows rose. "No?" He shook his head and finally shrugged. "Machines! They can never quite grasp the subtleties of human interaction, can they? That's what always gives us away."

She didn't believe for one moment that he'd interpreted her comment literally. He was, she realized with a touch of stunned amazement, amusing himself. "Let go of me," she said through gritted teeth.

His smile vanished. "I'm not even slightly tempted ... rogue hunter."

For the first time in her memory, Dalia felt real, unmitigated fear. "I wouldn't be fleeing the city if I were."

"The question is, *are* you fleeing the city? Or was this merely a clever ruse?"

She gave him a look. "I had my weapon on your back. I could've killed you then and there would've been no point in subterfuge."

"Except that that wouldn't have gotten you into the rebel camp, would it, Dalia?"

Dalia stared at him in dismay. She licked suddenly dry lips. "My name's Kaya."

"Your name is Dalia VH570 ... and you are a rogue hunter ... gone rogue."

Of all the things he might have said, nothing could have stunned her more, or more surely inspired her to throw caution to the wind. "I'm no rogue," she spat in disgust before she thought better of it. "I'm human."

His mouth tightened until his lips were no more than a thin line. His nostrils flared as he dragged in a deep breath to calm his temper. "You have enough contempt to be a rogue hunter, whatever you want to call yourself."

Dalia twisted, testing his hold of her, but she was not the least surprised when he held her without any sign of difficulty. She supposed she should have simply accepted the fact that she was dead except for the dying part. He knew she was a rogue hunter. He wasn't going to simply let her go, and he wasn't going to take her with him.

Somehow, though, she found she simply could not give up or accept that she wasn't going to be able to find a way out of this. "If you know about me, then you know I'm on the run. I'm no threat to you."

"Not presently. But, then, you're assuming I believe any propaganda the company chooses to put out. I don't." He leaned close, placing his mouth near her ear. "They lie," he whispered.

Her body obviously didn't know or care that he was a cyborg. The heat of his breath on her ear and his scent in her nostrils combined, sending a rush of heat and weakness through her that couldn't be interpreted as anything but desire.

An unaccustomed spurt of panic followed that confusing reaction. Dalia struggled to free her hands again. She was too much shorter than him, and too close, for a head butt to have any effect on him. More likely, she'd end up knocking herself out. Finding after only a few moments that she was having no appreciable effect, she desisted again, panting with effort. "What are you going to do with me?"

His arms tightened. Slowly, he lowered his head until his mouth was near her ear again. "Don't allow your prejudice to mislead you, little flower. I am not a machine. This flesh feels. This body desires. This mind wants. So, unless you want to discover what its like to spread your legs for a cyborg, I'd advise you to stop rubbing your very tantalizing little body against mine. I might decide to fuck you until no human *man* will ever do for you again."

Two completely polar sensations went through Dalia at once; outrage that he would even consider treating her--a trained warrior and rogue hunter--as if she was nothing more than a pleasure slave, and pretty much the same jolt of stunned attraction that had hit her the moment she saw him--except that this time it was accompanied by a rush of heat and a deluge of adrenaline.

She went perfectly still, more from shocked surprise than because he had commanded it, or because she feared he might keep his word, hardly daring even to breathe. As she stared up at him, however, it occurred to her that he had offered her a bargaining chip she hadn't even realized she possessed. "I would...." She licked her dried lips and tried again. "I will barter the use of my body for transport."

He frowned. "I would sooner leave you here. I'm sure it will surprise you, but I've no taste for killing ... and not much for humans, even to slake my needs."

Dalia felt blood flood her cheeks, only to wash away so rapidly she felt slightly dizzy. "But ... you said...."

"I lied."

She blinked at him, stunned once more, not because he admitted it, or even because he had the ability, but because he'd done it so convincingly that she'd believed him. It was no wonder the company had ceased production of this particular cyborg. It was no wonder he had never been caught. He was as human as any human spawned, but capable of far more than any human being, whether enhanced or not, and therefore far more dangerous.

"If you leave me here, you leave me to die," she said finally, trying to keep the desperation from her voice.

"Why?"

"Why what?"

"Assuming you're not lying and the company is hunting you, but not because you've gone rogue, then why?"

"I don't know."

He eyed her skeptically.

"I don't! I went in for my physical examination. When I woke, the tech was stabbing me with a needle."

He studied her for several moments and finally, slowly, released her. "You didn't question him?"

Dalia shrugged. "I snatched the needle out of my arm and drove it into his throat. It wasn't pretty, but it was fast. I didn't manage to get much out of him ... except...."

"Except?"

She shook her head. "Nothing that made any sense." She studied him for several moments and finally tried again. "Look, I know you've no reason to trust me, but it's only a matter of time before they catch up to me. I got rid of the locator--that's the only thing that's given me any time, but it won't last. Take me anywhere. As long as there's breathable air and half a chance for survival, I don't care. I'll give you everything I've got," she said, shoving the sleeve of her tunic up and extending her arm to show him her barcode.

He studied it, surprise flickering briefly across his features. He was frowning thoughtfully as he looked at her again. "You're coded."

"Everybody is coded at birth."

"Except cyborgs."

She studied him. "Cyborgs aren't born. They're created ... in a lab."

"Humans are created in labs," he countered, his lips tightening.

She thought about what the tech had told her and what she'd learned from the computer. "But not necessarily, and there's the difference. They have the ability to create life inside their own bodies. The tech ... before he died, he said that I was gestating. I have ... life, here," she finished, laying a hand over her lower belly.

He stared down at her hand for many moments before he looked up at her again. She had the sense that it was because he was so jolted by the admission that it took him far longer to assimilate the information than one would have expected. Shock was the human inability to accept what they had seen or heard, not something that should ever trouble a cyborg, a creation more machine than biological entity, regardless of their appearance or their artificial intelligence.

And still she had the feeling that he'd been as shocked as she had been at the news. He glanced away from her, turning his head to study something outside her range of vision. "They're coming."

Catching her arm just above the elbow, he led her up the gangplank and into the ship. They traversed a narrow corridor and finally arrived at the captain's cabin, which lay at the prow and encompassed the entire width of the ship. Pushing her inside, he studied her for several moments in silence. "You will stay here."

Chapter Four

Dalia counted four of them in all by the tread of their feet, as they came up the gangplank. Reuel met them at the top. No conversation was immediately exchanged, but she knew that Reuel was examining each with care to make certain they were whom they claimed to be.

Or, perhaps he knew them already? He'd said there was a rebel camp. The company had led her to believe that the rogues were, more or less, insane. Something had gone terribly wrong in their design. These cyborgs were a breed that had failed to perform as they had been intended and could not be controlled. They had to be hunted down and destroyed because they had either altered their CPU so that they could not be remotely destroyed, or the central processing unit itself had malfunctioned.

She supposed, willful disregard of their programming by deliberately reprogramming themselves was an act of rebellion, but what if there was more to it than that?

It seemed preposterous. According to what she had been told, the company had made no more than a thousand before they had discovered the defect and ceased production. As superior as these creations were to the race they had been designed to mimic, and even taking into consideration that they might, indeed, be insane, they could not, surely, expect to rebel openly against mankind and succeed?

And to what purpose, for that matter?

In truth, the line between the living human being and the cyborg had blurred as science progressed until the line that divided the two was often razor thin. Genetic manipulation, bioengineering and even mechanical enhancements were in widespread usage. Almost any naturally occurring human organ could be replaced by one that had been bio-engineered if need be. Missing, defective, or damaged body parts were as often as not replaced by cybornetic joints, limbs or digits.

The New Religion claimed cyborgs were an offense to their god, that they were soulless efforts of mortals at playing god. A soul was only created when those gifts of god, the seed of mankind, joined and began the process of growth. Only these were born with souls, and no matter how much of their bodies were replaced or enhanced, they still had souls. Animation was not life. Life created itself, propagated, replicated.

Why then had the tech said the life growing inside of her was not human? How could it be life and not be human? How was it even possible that she could maintain a life not human as she was?

For that matter, why and when and how had it been placed there to grow?

Rogue hunters were not encouraged to engage in sexual activities or to develop any sort of relationship for that matter. They were chosen to begin with because they had no familial attachments to distract them and they were discouraged from considering the possibility of doing so as long as they remained hunters. In point of fact, their training, which began before puberty, made it nearly impossible for them to form either emotional or physical attachments.

If that weren't enough, the penalty for breaking this 'law' was immediate termination, and the company made no bones about the fact that they were always under observation. The locator wasn't merely a device to keep track of their soldier's positions, or to find them in the event that they were wounded and unable to communicate. It recorded every move they made and reported everything they did.

Since she'd completed her training, she, herself, had never even felt the temptation to break this unwritten law. She was focused utterly on her missions. She had not engaged in any sexual activities, ever, not even with pleasure devises since she could see no sense in developing a taste for something she was forbidden to have anyway.

Therefore, there was no question in her mind that it had been placed there. What was not immediately apparent was the why and when.

The where was something that was almost as obvious as the how. It could not have occurred, she felt certain, anywhere except at the company's med lab. But why would the company do something that would jeopardize her usefulness as a hunter?

Assuming the spark of life clung, the organism would grow, according to what she had learned from the med lab computer. She would not be able to fight without risking the life of the organism, and her own life for that matter. As a parasitic type of organism, as it grew and its needs increased, it would integrate its own system so thoroughly with hers that it would, literally, be almost like ripping a part of herself loose to break its hold and could devastate her own system.

Of what use was a hunter who could not hunt?

Despite her value as a hunter, she knew that she was expendable as far as the company was concerned. The task she had been trained for also insured her death, sooner or later. The extensive training and biomechanical enhancements they'd paid for had been to extend her usefulness. Perhaps, though, they had conceived a project they considered even more useful?

But, if that was the case, why then destroy both her and the experiment? Wouldn't it have been just as effective to destroy the organism? Very likely she would have been no wiser, just as she hadn't known that they had placed it there to begin with.

That seemed to indicate that the company had not sanctioned the experiment. Someone within the company had decided to experiment without the company's knowledge or consent, and then they had realized that they must destroy the evidence.

That seemed far-fetched, but it still fit most of the facts she knew. It seemed the most logical answer.

If they had been completely unaware of the experiment, and therefore unaware of the perpetrator's efforts to conceal his crime by killing her, then they would have seen her act as murder, not self-defense. That was why they'd put out a sanction on her. They thought she'd gone mad, become dangerously unstable.

Unfortunately, there were a number of things that didn't seem to fit and most of it revolved around the incident in the examination room. The tech, it seemed to her, had found something he had not expected to find. Moreover, he was merely a lowly tech, no more than an assistant, certainly not educated or intelligent enough to have conceived or executed any sort of experiment on his own. He'd not taken it upon himself to destroy her. He'd been ordered by someone to do so.

There was another problem with her theory, as well. Ordinarily, she was only called upon to present herself for a physical examination directly before and directly after an assignment, the first to make certain she was in peek condition before she left, the second to repair any damage accruing from completion of her mission. Over the past four months, she had been called back repeatedly, however, each time for something supposedly minor that had been overlooked before, a test that had been badly performed and needed to be done again.

How could the company, who was rather a lot like the god the New Religion worshipped and knew all, have been unaware that experiments were being performed on her?

Finally, realizing that she didn't have nearly enough facts to fit all the puzzle pieces together--perhaps never would--she dismissed it and turned to study the captain's cabin.

It was luxurious enough to tell her several things about Reuel--he enjoyed the better things of life, liked his comfort, and he probably spent the better part of his time in this ship--or he was adept at stealing the better things in life and had an eye for quality.

The bed took up almost half the space and was certainly not typical of the bunks generally found on cruisers much less racers. On course, Reuel was massive--she should have known instantly that such magnificence was not naturally occurring--standing six foot four easily, probably a good three feet across the shoulders, his back, chest, arms, belly and legs taut and at the same time bulging with muscle.

The musculature would need to be massive, of course, and generally was in cyborgs because the alloy skeletal system was notably heavier than the calcium based skeletal structure of a human being, but Reuel was notable even among others of his kind, and the human males, hunters, that had been enhanced to track them.

There were only a handful of females like herself. Despite enhancements, they could not be made to be even nearly as strong as their male counterparts, and certainly not the cyborgs. Their strength was in disarming their quarry, which was also the reason there were only a few of them. If it became widely known that there were female hunters, their effectiveness would be diminished.

The thick carpet beneath her feet hummed as she wandered about the cabin, alerting her to the fact that the craft was preparing for departure. She moved to the chair before Reuel's desk and sat, strapping herself in, and then studied the charts on his desk briefly. She had no knowledge of navigation, however, and soon lost interest. Behind the desk were shelves containing row upon row of strange rectangular objects. As the humming increased to a tooth-rattling shake, she pulled one from the shelf and studied it, discovering that it was a very rare, ancient book of paper. There were few in existence any longer since they had not been produced in several hundred years, and many of those produced then had not been designed for the wear and tear of time. She'd seen them, though, in museums. She'd never actually touched one.

The first thing she noticed when she parted the pages was the smell. She held it a little closer, sniffing it, then sneezed. It smelled--more like dirt, she decided, than anything else, but also as if, over time, every smell around it had been absorbed into it and held so that it was such a collection of differing things as to make any single part unidentifiable.

It wasn't particularly pleasant. On the other hand, she didn't smell very pleasantly herself at the moment. It wasn't uncommon, in the field, for her to find herself without the facilities to bathe, but she had never grown accustomed to it, never been able to simply ignore being dirty and unkempt. As soon as the craft settled back into the smooth glide that told her it was safe to unbuckle herself, she placed the book back on the shelf, unfastened her restraints and got up to check out the facilities.

As she'd suspected, Reuel had his own, private, facilities. Doubtless, considering the size of the ship, the other cabins shared a community bath, but she supposed, if she was to remain in Reuel's cabin, that she would be allowed to make use of his. She intended to, in any event.

The stockings she'd taken had been little protection to begin with and had long since worn through. She tossed those into the incinerator unit. The trousers and tunic were in nearly as bad a shape, but she stuffed them into the cleaning unit before she climbed into the particle shower. To her stunned surprise, water shot from the jets, nearly drowning her when she gasped instinctively. Coughing and choking on the water she'd inhaled, she felt around blindly for some way to turn the thing off. She wasn't certain if she found it, though, or if the unit was designed to go on and off at five second intervals, for it did just that, startling her all over again the first few times.

Finally, she realized that the water itself was not supposed to clean her. There were cloths and some sort of thick gel-like chemical substance to rub on herself to remove the odor and dirt. The water was to remove the gel.

It seemed curiously inefficient. A particle shower would have cleaned and sanitized her in a matter of moments. Having to scrub herself was more of a job that she particularly cared for, and she wasn't convinced that she had been sanitized properly even when she was done.

She discovered she rather liked the way the water felt crawling over her bare skin, however. It felt--strange--but at the same time pleasurable. Finally, almost reluctantly, she got out of the unit and discovered two not very pleasant side effects. Scrubbing her hair had felt good, but it had left it in a wet, tangled mess. Moreover, the water still ran down her body and dripped off onto the carpeted floor.

Rain had a similar effect and since she'd been on many worlds unprotected by domes from nature, she knew from experience that neither her skin nor her hair would dry very quickly.

She was still standing in front of the unit wondering whether to put her clothing back on as she was or to stand where she was and wait until she dried when the door opened. She jumped reflexively, whirling to face the threat.

Reuel stood in the opening, surveying her with interest from the top of her head to her bare toes. Finally, he leaned casually against the frame, folding his arms over his chest as if he was getting comfortable to stay a while. "I see you figured out how to use the shower unit," he said after a moment.

Dalia shifted uncomfortably from one foot to the other, uneasy with his curious interest for no reason that she could immediately perceive. There was nothing threatening in his stance. "I think so," she said a little doubtfully.

His brows rose. "But you're not certain?"

"I've never used anything but a particle bath. I didn't even know there was such a thing as this water bath. Is it something new?"

His lips curled in a half smile. Oddly, her belly clenched as she looked at it. "It's something very old--ancient--from the age of decadence."

Her eyes widened. "Then it is outlawed."

Chuckling, he stood away from the door and pulled his tunic over his head. Dalia was so surprised by the sound of his laughter, by the amusement it conveyed as well as the pleasure the sound sent through her, that he'd tugged his boots off and discarded them, as well, before she realized that he fully intended to remove all of his clothes. "I am a rogue, little flower. Why would I concern myself over the laws of man?"

Dalia swallowed with an effort, so mesmerized by the strength and fluidity of his movements, by the sheer beauty of his body, that her mind as well as her eyes were focused completely upon what he was doing, leaving very little room for other thought. Why and how, she wondered, could merely looking at him have such a ... consuming effect upon her?

It was more than the perception of beauty. Anything pleasing to the eye was likely to capture her attention, but certainly not so completely that she lost track of all else.

When he'd removed his trousers, she saw that his lower body was as fascinating as the upper part. His hips were narrow so that his broad chest formed almost a V shape, his legs powerful. He also, for no reason that immediately came to mind, possessed a phallus, and not merely for the sake of appearing to be a male creature. It stood proudly erect above a pair of testicles, sprouting from a nest of dark hair.

She hadn't noticed it before and she knew damn well she would have noticed something that--enormous. It functioned, at least in the sense that it acted like the erectile tissue on a human counterpart.

Why would a cyborg that had never been designed or intended as a pleasure droid, have been so faithfully reproduced as a man, complete with testicles and an obviously fully functional--make that massive--phallus?

She was so enthralled by the sight of it that it wasn't until he moved so close that she lost sight of it that she realized he was moving toward her.

She dragged her gaze upward to his face as he stopped in front of her, noticing every inch of flesh, every bugle, ripple, hair follicle and even the texture of his skin, on the way up.

Whoever had designed him, she realized suddenly, and with perfect clarity, had fully intended to create man, not just a facsimile of man. Whoever had created him had been playing god--and it seemed very likely that whoever it was, was the same 'god' who had decided to experiment on her. Was that what the tech had meant when he'd said it wasn't human? Had Reuel's creator decided to go one step further and see if he could mimic the creation of life through reproduction and birth?

Without a word he caught her shoulders, turned her toward the shower unit, and urged her inside, following her.

She turned to face him as the water jetted over her, covering her face. When it ceased to pelt them, he moved away, took the cloth and rubbed the chemical substance into it until he had created a lather. Then calmly, almost methodically, he began to rub the cloth over her body, gliding it over first one arm and then the other, then turning her and rubbing it along her back and buttocks. Instead of urging her to turn once more when he'd finished lathering her back, he stepped up closely behind her, so closely she could feel his flesh brushing against hers with each movement, and reached around her to lather her breasts and belly.

Dalia remained perfectly still, at first because she was surprised, both by his actions and by his gentleness, and also because she wasn't at all certain where she stood with this dangerous rogue. Surprise gave way to something entirely different, however, as she felt his hands glide over her breasts. Her nipples puckered and stood erect, as if she was cold, except she wasn't. A strange current flowed from the tips of her breasts through her body, creating an odd sort of expectancy inside her, an involuntary tensing of muscles and, at the same time, a diminishing of tension, creating heat. She dragged in a ragged breath, not certain whether she wanted him to stop or continue as a drugging sort of lassitude swept over her. Slowly, he worked the cloth downward, finally cupping his hand over her femininity, parting her nether lips and delving into the cleft, tracing it.

Dalia's belly clenched almost painfully. She swallowed with an effort, licked her lips. "What are you doing?"

"Teaching you," he murmured, his voice sounding strangely hoarse, "the finer points of bathing with soap and water."

Dalia's knees almost buckled, dumping her on the floor of the shower unit, as he stepped away from her abruptly, allowing the shower to pelt the soap from her body. Cool air wafted over her as he opened the door of the unit and stepped out.

Frowning, shivering more from reaction than from the chill draft of air, she sloughed as much water from her body as she could with her hands and stepped out, as well. He'd opened a cabinet in the wall, she saw. He pulled a sheet of fabric from it, tossed it to her, then pulled another one out and began to rub it over himself, soaking up the excess water on his skin.

She scrubbed the cloth he'd thrown to her over her own skin and discovered that it was reasonably effective. Her skin still felt damp, but only a little. Her hair continued to drip even after she'd scrubbed the towel over it. Reuel's black hair was nearly as long as her own, falling well past his shoulders, so she watched him to see what he would do with his own hair.

He merely rubbed it with the cloth to remove as much water as possible, raked a comb through it to remove the tangles and left it to drip. Shrugging, she combed the snarls from her own hair and left the bath with cold rivulets of water trickling unpleasantly down her back.

He was standing before an open locker in the room, pulling clothing from it, she saw. Turning, he tossed a tunic to her. She caught it, but studied it doubtfully. The clothes she'd stolen before had been too big. Any tunic that would cover his body was unlikely to even remotely fit her.

Mentally shrugging, she pulled it on and discovered she hadn't mistaken the matter. The tunic fell almost to her knees. The neck opening gaped and the sleeves completely covered her hands.

When he'd finished dressing, he turned to study her. His lip quirked upward on one side. Striding toward her, he caught the fabric in his hands and ripped first one sleeve and then the other from the tunic. She rather thought it might have worked better, however, if she'd merely rolled the sleeves up. The shoulders drooped well down her upper arms and the armholes ended in the general vicinity of her waist. The sides of her breasts were fully exposed and the whole breast threatened to fall out the sides when she moved.

She studied the effect doubtfully.

"We are machines, not men. You needn't concern yourself that any will be so overcome with lust over your human body as to accost you," he said dryly.

Chapter Five

A combination of anger and discomfort brought color forward to tinge Dalia's cheeks. Obviously, she had gravely insulted him when she'd allowed him to see how revolting she considered the idea of copulating with a cyborg. He seemed determined to emphasize the fact that he was a cyborg at every opportunity, at the same time giving it the lie by proving that he was far more than a 'mere' machine. He was not imitating the reaction of a human to an insult. Clearly, he had felt it. She wondered if his creators realized just how far beyond machines these cyborgs had evolved. She supposed they must if they considered them so dangerous. "It hadn't occurred to me that it would be a problem," she responded tightly. "I was only thinking that it was not very comfortable."

She could tell by the expression on his face that he knew she was lying.

Was he truly as unique as he seemed? Or had the others she'd destroyed been as he was?

It disturbed her to think they might have been. She had refused to consider that they were anything more than machines, very impressive machines, the cutting edge of technology, but still no different, really, than any other machine when all was said and done. Cutting them down was no different than destroying ... a refrigerating unit, for instance. Except they bled, and the blood gave her nightmares and the look of despair in their artificial eyes as they died gave her nightmares.

If she had not known that strangely beautiful, and very unforgettable, face from the bulletins that had been posted on him, she was doubtful that she would ever have realized that he was not human, and that disturbed her almost as much as the other. How many, she wondered, walked undetected among them? Infiltrating every aspect of their society, possibly preparing to strike down their creators before their creators could destroy them?

Grasping her upper arm, he led her from the cabin and down the narrow passage that bisected the ship. When they reached a stairwell, he pushed her in front of him. Grasping the handrail, she preceded him and found herself in a large room that was obviously intended as a social room. Here comfortably stuffed chairs were arranged in small groupings.

Four pairs of cyborg eyes turned as she entered, examining her with what she could only describe as-- interest, curiosity, even a touch of hostility. There was no cool, emotionless appraisal, not from one. There was no similarity between them beyond a general physical build, height and weight. Two were blond, two dark, but the shades varied drastically, as did their eye color and facial features, but then she hadn't expected them to look as if they'd come off of an assembly line. They had arisen from a new generation of cyborg, and had been touted as 'each as uniquely different and natural as a real, live human.' It was one of the things that had made tracking them down extremely difficult. They had been designed to blend in with humans.

"We have a hunter among us. She is ... mine. I will expect you to remember that and act accordingly."

The cyborgs had stiffened at Reuel's announcement, several of them half rising from their seats. They settled back, their expressions more guarded than before.

"You're not taking her to the camp?"

"Why did you bring her?"

"Why didn't you kill her?"

"For what purpose have you brought her among us?"

They spoke almost at once, each question spilling over the question of another, tangling so that it was hard to separate them.

"When I understand myself ... when, and if, I feel the urge to share, I will tell you," Reuel said coldly. "Until then, it is not your right ask."

"You endanger us all, risk the failure of our plans by bringing her among us. That should give us the right."

Reuel moved to a chair near the others and sat. Wrapping an arm around Dalia's waist, he pulled her down onto his lap. She resisted, for all the good it did, sitting stiffly erect. He wouldn't allow even that much rebellion, however. He pulled her against him and held her until she relaxed, dropping her head back against his shoulder. "You see this tiny morsel of mortal flesh as a threat?" he said, his voice deep, husky.

"That is the huntress, Dalia. She has killed almost as many as the other hunters together," one of the cyborgs growled.

Almost casually, Reuel slipped a hand through the arm opening of her tunic and began to pluck at her nipple with his thumb and forefinger. Dalia stiffened, tried to jerk upright, but his grip tightened until she relaxed once more with the realization that she could not free herself, could not move until he allowed it. Swallowing with an effort, she fixed her gaze across the room, trying to ignore his touch, trying to ignore the fact that the other cyborgs had been instantly riveted by his actions. "This delicate little flower?" he insisted, rolling the distended nipple between his finger and thumb. "I'm afraid I find it difficult to perceive her as a threat--at least, not in the way that you mean."

Dalia was relieved when he finally released her nipple-- until he slipped his hand down her belly and cupped her sex. She clamped her legs tightly. Abandoning that goal after only a moment, he slid his hand up her belly and caught her other nipple between his thumb and forefinger, plucking at it until it stood erect and began to throb like an aching tooth.

"If we were men, now, that might be a different matter altogether," he murmured, his husky voice almost as mesmerizing as the teasing caress of his hand. "She is a wondrous marvel of nature, don't you think? Even I can understand how a man, who is still slave to his hormonal urges, would find himself distracted and vulnerable because of it."

Almost casually, he lifted his legs, one at the time, and propped the heels of his boots on the table that separated the chairs. As he did so, her legs slid off on either side of his. She scarcely noticed. She was so enthralled by his touch, and trying desperately to ignore the sensations shimmying through her that she hardly noticed when he removed the arm that was around her waist and slipped his opposite hand through her tunic. He cupped her breast in his hand, massaging it even as he plucked gently, rhythmically at the nipple.

She'd lost track of the other hand, the one he'd been teasing her with before. When it skated over her belly, the muscles there jumped, clenched. This time when his hand settled between her legs, she discovered she could not clamp her legs together. She tried, reflexively.

Apparently completely unconcerned, possibly even unaware, of her attempts to prevent his incursion, he used his fingers to part the petals of flesh and slid one large finger along her cleft. Dalia thought for several moments that she would faint. She was struggling so hard to keep her breathing regular, to still the frantic drum of her heart, that she kept holding her breath.

"As a machine, naturally I'm incapable of feeling ... anything at all, but I do find this female interesting to study. This, for instance," he said, pushing her tunic aside and displaying the breast he held in his hand, "is interestingly symmetrical. The color and texture is also interesting in that the shading of the flesh contrasts so sharply from here," he massaged her breast, "to here," he plucked the distended nipple.

For the first time since he'd begun to toy with her, Dalia looked at the cyborgs across from them. Any doubt that she'd ever entertained that lust was a concept beyond their capability or understanding vanished. They were, quite obviously, as enthralled by what Reuel was doing to her as she was, and, strangely enough, she lost the vague sense of discomfort that had been nibbling at the back of her mind.

As if something had broken inside of her--all urge to fight it--she released a shaky breath that was half gasp, half groan as she felt him push the finger he'd been exploring her sex with up inside of her.

The groan that escaped her had the unexpected effect of making him cease abruptly, though he seemed to withdraw that probing finger almost reluctantly. Removing his hands from inside the tunic, he smoothed it over her. "If we were men, we would lust for this female, allow it to blind us to danger, and reason, and then ... only then, would this small mortal be a threat to us," he growled, dropping his feet to the deck and pushing her off his lap abruptly.

She stood shakily, staring down at him in confusion. He surged to his feet, grasped her arm as he had before and half pushed, half dragged her from the room and up the stairs. Reaching his cabin once more, Dalia turned on him as he closed the door behind them. "Why did you do that?"

His face hardened. "Did it bother you? Surely, it didn't ...being fondled by a machine, in front of more machines. You should have thought no more of it than if I were some mechanical pleasure devise, and they were ... furniture."

Her lips tightened. "You've made your point, many times over. I still want to know why."

He moved toward her until he was looming over her. "Because it pleased me to do it. Because you are mine and I will do as I please with you at any time it pleases me to do it. So that *you* would know your danger. So that *they* would know that you are mine and I would kill them if they so much as looked at you." He stopped, dragged in a ragged breath. "And because I couldn't stop myself once I'd started."

He gripped her arms, pulling her up against him until her breasts flattened against his chest, then slipped an arm behind her back and caught her face in his other hand. "Is this how you did it, my deadly little flower? Did you allow them to think that you looked upon them as men? Did you sigh and moan at their touch as if you enjoyed it, waiting until their minds were so heated with need that it was easy for you to slip a blade into their heart?"

Dalia swallowed with an effort. "No!" she said shakily. "It would never have occurred to me! I wasn't trained to do such a thing and I would never have let them near enough to me to try it. I didn't even know it was possible. I bested them."

He studied her face carefully. Finally, a dark eyebrow rose skeptically. "Toe to toe, in combat?"

She flushed. "I outwitted them, caught them by surprise. I'm skilled in the usage of all weapons and hand to hand combat. Yes, it was considered that I wouldn't be perceived as a threat because I'm a female and not physically threatening in appearance, but no one considered, least of all me, that it was even possible to ... lure a cyborg to his death."

"Least of all you."

Dalia licked her lips nervously. "You're not going to let me go, are you?"

The movement of her tongue seemed to distract him. After a moment, he lifted his gaze to hers. "Probably not."

"If you were going to kill me, you might as well have done it before we left."

"I've no taste for killing. I told you that."

"But you have killed, haven't you?"

He didn't even flinch. "I have."

Dalia frowned. "If you're not going to kill me and you're not taking me to the rebel camp, what do you plan to do with me?"

His grip on her relaxed, allowing her to slip down his chest until she was no longer standing on her toes. His lip quirked upward at one corner, but unlike before, the smile didn't touch his eyes. "For the moment I'm merely trying to decide whether or not the risk is worth taking you up on your offer."

"Which offer?" she asked, feeling a sinking of dread.

"The use of your body in return for safe passage. Money is not something difficult to acquire. A willing female-- human female--is a little more rare."

Chapter Six

"You hate me," Dalia said in sudden enlightenment.

He released her abruptly. "Droids are incapable...."

"But you aren't a Droid. You hate me for being a good soldier."

"I don't hate you for being good at what you were designed to do. If I did, I would have killed you and left your body for the company to find."

Dalia stared at him. "You hate them worse. You didn't because you didn't want to do them any favors."

Something flickered in his eyes then and she knew she had at least part of the answer. "True, but then I could have left you unidentifiable."

That seemed inarguable. She was no weakling. She was capable of doing things that no normal women, and even few men, were capable of because of her mechanical enhancements, and yet his strength was so superior to her own she was as helpless as if she'd had no enhancements at all. "You still could," she said, wondering why she felt the need or desire to test him, wondering if she was goading him.

"I still might."

She didn't believe him and relief flooded through her. Whatever else his plans for her might be, she was as certain as she could be that he had no plans to kill her.

The other cyborgs were another matter, of course. She'd seen the look in their eyes and it went way past hostility. He might not hate her for who she was and what she was, but they almost certainly did ... and if he took her to the rebel camp, then there could be hundreds there who felt the same way as they did.

She moistened her lips. "But not before you find out why the company considers me a threat?"

"Not before that," he said coolly. He glanced around the cabin. "I would suggest you spend most of your time in the cabin. I don't believe they will challenge me, but ... you will not wish to stake your life on it. We eat at O eight hundred, twelve hundred, and eighteen hundred, in the mess, no exceptions. Lights out at twenty three hundred. Otherwise, do as you please. So long as I don't catch you near anything of significant military importance or attempting to sabotage the ship, you can move around the ship if you prefer it."

She was on the point of asking him where he intended to sleep, or if he even found it necessary, but she thought better of it. She, for one, was convinced, and she had no desire to endure any more lessons. Whatever the company thought, these cyborgs were not 'mere' machines with artificial intelligence. They were, in effect, a higher order of beings, superior to humans because mankind had been foolish enough to make them so.

When he'd left, her shoulders slumped and absolute weariness set in. She'd hardly slept since she'd escaped, knowing if she allowed herself to sleep deeply the chances were good that she wouldn't get the chance to wake up. She was also hungry, but according to the clock set into the wall, it was twenty four hundred--there would be no chance for food before morning.

Dismissing it, she decided she was more tired anyway and climbed onto the bed. She'd barely settled in a comfortable position when she dropped from consciousness as suddenly as if a switch had been turned off. Despite that, she didn't rest a lot easier than she had in the rubble of the buildings, expecting any moment to be discovered. Strange, heated dreams kept her moving restlessly throughout the night. Again and again, she relived those moments when Reuel's hands had slipped over her body. Sometimes it differed. Sometimes they were in the shower and he was lathering her with soap. Sometimes they lay entwined in the bed.

When she woke, she discovered that he was lying beside her on his back, staring up at the bulkhead. She had the uneasy feeling that he had not 'rested', but had no idea of how long he'd lain beside her. Uncomfortable with the dreams that had plagued her most of the night, she rose without a word and went into the head. Discarding the tunic she'd slept in, she removed the clothing she'd taken from the clinic from the cleaning unit and dressed. When she left the head, Reuel was gone.

Hunger drove her from the cabin. She found the mess by following the smell of food. The cyborgs, she discovered were more punctual than she. When she arrived, all of them, including, she saw with relief, Reuel, were seated at the long table in the middle of the room. All of them except Reuel were wearing their weapons, but they seemed far too interested in consuming their food for her to consider that circumstance as representing a threat ... for the moment at least.

Mentally, she shrugged. At rest, they were basically like their human counterparts. They used very little energy. However, physically, they were at least three quarters pure biological material, most of it muscle, and moving all of that around required a great deal of energy. Even if they didn't have the human tendency to eat purely for entertainment and pleasure, consuming what they needed would require a great deal of food.

Selecting her own food from the server, she moved down the table and sat next to Reuel. Even without the 'lesson' or 'experiment'--whatever name Reuel cared to put to the display the day before--she would've been uneasy about being in a room full of cyborgs. The surreptitious, speculative glances she'd noticed as she moved around the mess hall had only increased that natural tendency.

All things considered, it occurred to her to wonder if the shortage of females would prove to be a problem for the cyborg community--she assumed it was a community. To her knowledge, not even a third of the rogue cyborgs were female and since they weren't as strong as their male counterparts, the hunters had decreased that by a goodly number since they'd gone rogue. A fraction of this generation, mostly female, had been reprogrammed as soon as the first ones had gone rogue. As far as she could see that left anywhere from three to five males to every female-- assuming they'd managed to gather the remainder together.

It seemed unlikely that they had. She was willing to admit that she'd had a great deal of prejudice where this generation of cyborgs, the CO469, were concerned, mostly because of the company's propaganda machine. As the blond with the curly hair had pointed out, though, she'd taken her fair share of them down. Taking a cyborg down was no simple task, however. Typically, she spent months tracking and then studying the subject before she devised a plan--only a fool leapt in with guns blazing when they were facing a foe as potentially dangerous as these rogues.

She had seen nothing to make her believe the CO469 were that much different than the generations before or since them. Either this particular phenomenon she'd witnessed since she'd been taken aboard Reuel's ship was rare even among them, or the ones she'd killed had actually been 'acting', or, possibly, whatever it was that made these so very human had had the effect of actually making some of them truly insane.

It was possible, of course, that those she'd tracked had been on some sort of mission for the rebels, but she was more inclined to think they'd been loners and knew nothing about the rebels.

None had ever admitted it, in any case, which certainly seemed to whittle at the numbers the rebels might have put together. If she added to that the difficulties that seemed inevitable given the shortage of females and the all too obvious instincts of the males to try to find a female to breed with, it looked like a recipe for disaster to her.

She supposed, given that the CO469 was particularly partial to attacking the company and had yet to focus on anyone or anything else, provided it didn't get in their way, she could see the company's stance where they were concerned. By law, they were responsible for removing potentially hazardous or defective product anyway, but she began to feel that there was more to it than that.

Their fear seemed excessive now that she thought about it. Either they knew they'd crossed the line and created a generation of cyborgs that were as close to human as made almost no difference at all, or there was something about these cyborgs that was potentially far more dangerous than their relatively small number suggested.

The question was what?

And was it possible that it was in any way connected to what had happened to her?

She wouldn't have thought so except for Reuel's interest.

If she hadn't been half starved from lack of food, dehydrated from little water and dead on her feet, she would've realized that she'd 'surprised' Reuel with amazing ease. Of course, she hadn't realized until she was upon him that he was a cyborg--she wouldn't have known it then except that she'd seen his face so many times she would've had to be a blithering idiot not to recognize him instantly.

He had not been suffering any of the debilitating effects that she had, however, and his vision and hearing were many times more acute than her own. If he'd been human, as she had supposed, she wouldn't have questioned whether or not she'd actually managed to sneak up on him. She should have questioned it the moment she'd recognized him, because it was very unlikely that she'd caught Reuel off guard.

He'd been waiting for her.

She should've known finding that 'guide' had been too goddamned easy!

She didn't know how much Reuel knew that he wasn't telling her, but she was about to find out.

Snatching the saber from the scabbard of the man sitting next to her, she leapt upward almost in the same motion, landing on the table, the point of her blade hovering just above where Reuel's heart would be if he did as she expected and leapt to his feet.

He didn't disappoint her.

Behind her, she heard the scrapes and crashes that told her the others had leapt up, turning their chairs over as they grabbed their weapons. Silence fell as they froze, just as Reuel had frozen. "It was a set up," she said through gritted teeth. "You were waiting for me."

Instead of answering her immediately, Reuel's gaze flicked to the cyborgs behind her. "Get back. This is between me and her."

Listening, she heard them shift indecisively. Finally, they moved back a couple of steps. None of them moved far, however, and none left.

It didn't matter. She was going to die anyway. She rather thought she liked these odds better than the odds she'd be facing if she let them get her all the way to the rebel camp. Five to one might not be much of a chance, but it was better than 500 to one. "What's the game plan, Reuel?" she demanded, prodding him with the point of the saber.

"I was waiting," he admitted.

"Why? How?"

"We're plugged into the company's system. We monitor all of their activities."

"So you knew they were after me and you knew the sector of the city where they'd lost me. They were out looking for me?" she asked, jerking her head in the direction of the cyborgs behind her.

Her overconfidence cost her. She'd been so certain the threat was behind her, she hadn't realized that Reuel was only waiting for a fraction of a second's inattention. The moment she nodded in the direction of the cyborgs at her back, her gaze flickered away from his. He struck the side of the blade in her hands so hard with the palm of his hand that the vibration traveled all the way up her arm in a numbing shockwave. She leapt from the table even as he made a dive for her. Landing on the deck in a half crouch, she pivoted so that she was facing both Reuel and the others.

One of them--the blond that had given her the evil eye from the time they'd boarded--snatched his saber from its scabbard and tossed it to Reuel. Reuel caught it, but it seemed a more reflexive action than intentional. He glanced down at the saber as if undecided whether to keep it or discard it. Dalia made a lunging swing at him while he was distracted.

He parried it, but again she sensed that it was an instinctive action of self-preservation.

She didn't have time to dwell on it, or figure it out. The only chance she had that she could see would be to take him out. The corner of the room where she'd positioned herself ensured that no more than one or two of them could come at her at once, while still giving her enough room to maneuver.

It wasn't much of a chance, but it was better than nothing.

As Reuel rolled from the table and landed on his feet, she swung again. Again, he met the swing, parried it, but he made no attempt to follow it up. He moved to one side, trying to force her to move further into the opening. She wasn't falling for that one, however. She held her position, attacking once more in a flurry of strikes that forced him back.

The numbness in her arm from that first hit had subsided, leaving pain in its wake. She shifted the blade to her other hand, hoping the pain would recede enough that she could switch back. She was almost as good with her left hand as her right, but almost, she felt sickeningly certain, wasn't going to be good enough.

Parrying her strikes, he shifted again, moving to her other side. Again, she faced him, refusing to allow him to work her out of the corner, but his new position made it necessary for her to switch hands again.

He'd seen the weakness, she realized with dread, switching, gritting her teeth and trying to ignore the pain. This time, instead of merely meeting her thrusts, he launched an attack. Dalia met the flurry of strikes, but she was forced to give ground inch by inch. At almost the same moment she realized he'd forced her into the corner, she lost her death grip on her saber.

He swung, she parried, but the shock wave that went through her arm paralyzed her fingers. Her blade went flying across the room. She watched its path, expecting to feel the bite of his blade any moment.

Instead, to her surprise, he tossed his sword aside, grabbed her arms and pinned them behind her back. He was breathing almost as heavily as she was, but she had the distinct feeling it had little to do with either fear or exertion. His expression was as black as a thundercloud.

"Secure the weapons," he growled through clenched teeth without bothering to turn his head. "The next man I see wearing one is a dead man."

Securing both her wrists in one hand, he urged her forward by lifting up on her arms until she had to lean forward, or move, to ease the pressure.

"Do I make myself clear?" he demanded in a growl as he faced the others.

The two nearest the door saluted and left abruptly. The two who remained collected the sabers from the floor, saluted, and departed behind the others. Without a word, Reuel pushed her toward the door and down the corridor. When they reached his cabin, he dragged her over to the locker at the foot of his bed and opened it. The scrape of metal against metal caught Dalia's attention. She turned in time to see him pull a length of chain from the locker. On either end was a manacle.

The moment he clamped one around her wrist, she wrenched free of him and swung the chain, which had a manacle on the other end, as well, at his head. He caught it mid-air. Wincing, he grasped her around the waist and tossed her backwards. She landed on the bed with a bounce. The mattress, soft and yielding, cushioned her fall, but it also hampered her effort to gain a stance that would allow her to launch another attack. Before she could right herself, he launched himself at her. The impact laid her out flat, stunning her.

Straddling her, he sat upright, grasped her free hand and clamped the manacle around it, then caught the chain in the middle and secured it to a bolt in the bulkhead above the head of the bed.

Dalia jerked her head upward to stare at the bolt, tugging on the chain, but she had a bad feeling that both the chain and the bolt had been made with her in mind and that she would have little chance of freeing herself from it.

Reuel grasped her face in one hand, pinching her cheeks as he forced her to look at him. "Don't ... ever ... try ... anything ... like ... that ... again," he said through clenched teeth, enunciating each word slowly and carefully.

"Afraid it'll make you look bad in front of your men?" she spat at him as the shock wore off and anger and frustration surged through her again.

"Because I'm afraid you'll hurt my child, you little fool," he ground out.

Chapter Seven

Dalia stared at Reuel blankly while dozens of questions crashed in on her, too many and too rapidly for her to give voice even to one. "Yours?" she gasped, feeling the shock give way to fury. "Yours! You son of a bitch!" she screamed, heaving upwards suddenly in an attempt to buck him off.

She caught him by surprise, surprised herself when she succeeded and he fell off of her sideways. Drawing her knees up, she kicked at him, landing both feet flat in the middle of his chest and shoving him backwards on the bed. He caught himself as he rolled toward the edge, grabbing her ankles ... or rather the legs of her trousers. To her surprise and his, the trousers slipped from her waist and he rolled off onto the floor, taking her trousers with him.

Growling, he leapt to his feet and dove for her again. She managed to get one knee and one foot planted against his chest, but it was an awkward position and didn't give her enough leverage to launch him. He grasped her knees, forcing them apart and wedged himself between her legs.

Panting, she glared at him in furious silence.

He glared back at her.

"That's what he meant when he said it wasn't human," she said tightly, discovering to her horror that she suddenly felt curiously close to tears.

Some of the anger left his face, but the emotions that flickered in his eyes confused her--hurt, relief, pride in quick succession. Before she could question him further, he shifted upward, covering her mouth with his own in a kiss that was both possessive and angry.

Surprise held her still. A confusion of sensations immersed her in an unbreakable grip, undermining the anger that lingered, or perhaps magnified by the adrenaline pumping through her that her anger had produced. His mouth was hot, seductive, as was his tongue as he forced it between her surprised lips and raked it across her own, inducing a response that encompassed her entire body as his taste and scent filled her. She struggled against it, fought to hold to her anger and supplant the temptation to fall under his spell, writhing and bucking against him, trying to twist her face away and break the kiss.

Her efforts only seemed to incite him. He ceased his exploration of her mouth and began to thrust his tongue in and out rhythmically, mimicking the thrust and retreat of the sexual act with his tongue and her mouth. The motion, his taste, and the imagery he evoked, combined to drown the last ounce of willpower from her, supplanting her anger with a growing sense of desperation. She closed her mouth around his tongue, sucking him.

Her response shattered the last vestiges of his control. Wrenching his mouth from hers, he grasped the neck of her tunic with both hands and parted it as if it had been no more substantial than paper. Dalia gasped. The moment he covered her breast with his mouth, however, she completely lost track of any protest she might have thought to make. The heat of his mouth, the teasing nudge of his tongue evoked much the same response from her body as his fingers had when he had teased her before, except many times over. Her head swam. She had to struggle to draw breath into her lungs. Her awareness narrowed to focus on the sensations rioting through her and little else.

Frustration surfaced, briefly, when she discovered her restraints prevented her from either holding him to her or thrusting him away, and she was of two minds about which she wanted worse. The powerful sensations tearing through her as he moved his mouth from one breast to the other, teasing her, lathing her with his tongue, nipping her with the edge of his teeth were almost beyond bearing, but neither did she think she could stand it if he stopped.

"Reuel," she gasped his name, in supplication, reaching a point at last where she felt she would die if he didn't stop so she could catch her breath. "Don't! Please!"

For a moment, she thought he was deaf to her pleas. Slowly, he lifted his head and his gaze locked with hers. She swallowed with an effort, feeling her body cry out with demand the moment he ceased to tease her. "Oh god! Don't stop!"

His features contorted, almost, it seemed, with pain. Leaning toward her, he covered her mouth with his own once more, kissing her deeply, almost savagely, as he slipped a hand between their bodies and traced the cleft of her sex, parting the flesh, testing the exquisitely sensitive inner surfaces with the tip of his finger and sending excruciating shock waves through her that made her belly clench painfully. She rocked her hips, moving against his hand, urging him to penetrate her body. A groan of pleasure clawed its way up her throat when he did.

He probed her with his thick forefinger only a moment, however. Disappointment filled her when he withdrew it. In the next moment, she felt something far larger probing her in its place. She arched toward him eagerly, aiding his descent into her depths as he stretched her woman's passage with his engorged phallus, filling her slowly. His claiming sent waves of escalating passion through her, lifting her to new heights when she'd thought she could not feel more, enjoy more, bear any more without shattering, fainting, dying.

Twisting her wrists, she gripped the chain as he withdrew and drove into her once more. He caught her hips, holding her as he withdrew and thrust deeply inside her again, and again in almost a frenzy of deep, stabbing thrusts. She met him with a fervor that matched or surpassed his, feeling the tension build inside of her until, abruptly, it began to disintegrate, breaking apart in an eruption that poured heat and pleasure through her like lava, making the walls of her sex clench and unclench like a fisting hand around his phallus.

He shuddered, growling hoarsely as her body clenched around him, milking him of his fluids, arching jerkily as his body was caught up in the throes of release. When it subsided at last, he collapsed against her for several moments, gathering his strength. Finally, he pushed himself off of her with an effort and landed beside her on the bed. Rolling to his back, he dropped an arm across his eyes as he struggled to catch his breath.

Weak in the aftermath, so sated she could not think and had no wish to, Dalia melted against the bed and felt as if she was sinking into it as darkness swarmed around her. Inside, her body still quaked and twitched, as if tiny electric currents were discharging. Gradually, almost reluctantly, the tremors subsided, her heart slowed, and her lungs ceased to labor to drag in air.

The questions ebbed around her once more, like the whispers of distant voices. As before, they tripped over one another, merged, tangled her mind in confusion. The anger had vanished. She didn't know whether it was because he had so sated her with pleasure or if the anger had had no foundation to begin with. She turned her head to study him. "Why? Only tell me why, so I can understand."

He sat up abruptly, putting his back to her as he sat on the edge of the bed, scrubbing his hands over his face. "Give me your word you won't do anything that would jeopardize your life or the life of the child, and I will release you."

Impatience wove its way through her. "Not until I understand this."

He stood abruptly, adjusting his clothing as he turned to look at her. It was only then that she realized he hadn't even taken the time to undress himself. It occurred to her that she should've been repulsed at the almost primal way they had coupled, but even the explosive savagery of it in memory made her body clench all over again with remembered pleasure.

He shook his head, his lips tightening. "Emotion isn't a gift. It's a curse, a weakness we would have been better without. I should not have told you as much as I did--not yet. You're not ready."

His comments only confused her more. "I *am* ready."

He leaned toward her, bracing his arms on the bed. "If you were ready, you would not have flung it in my face as if it was a thing of such revulsion that ... never mind."

"I can't accept what I don't understand," she flung at him as he stood away from the bed and strode toward the door.

He paused there, turning to study her. For several moments, she thought he would say nothing else. Finally, he spoke.

"You are my Eve, Dalia, my curse and my salvation."

Chapter Eight

"What does that mean?" Dalia demanded as he closed the door behind him. She listened, but all she heard was his retreating footsteps. "Fuck!"

She pulled at the chain in frustration for several moments and finally subsided.

She should have told him what he wanted to hear, she realized irritably. He would've freed her. She'd been too focused on demanding answers, however--still too disoriented from what had happened between them to think clearly.

She settled back after a moment, knowing it was useless to struggle and still too weak, for that matter, to arouse enough strength even for anger. What had he meant, she wondered? His Eve?

It was a name, vaguely familiar, but she couldn't grasp the significance of it without knowing the origins. Frowning, she concentrated on activating the CPU assist implanted in her skull, referencing the word as a word first, and then as a name when she decided it could have nothing to do with time ... unless he meant twilight? The end of life?

She dismissed that and summoned the other data. Faces flashed before her eyes, biographies, history. She discarded them, one after another. Finally, the computer referenced a defunct religion from several centuries earlier. Eve was the name given to the first woman--the woman created for the first man, Adam--according to that religion, and from them the human race had sprung. She had been designed to be his companion and mate, and she had so enthralled him that he'd allowed her to lead him astray.

The reference only left her more confused, not less so. Had he meant it in that context? Or had he meant something else?

She could not have been created for him, not in the truest sense. She was human and he wasn't. Perhaps it was a poetic reference? He had said she was his, had claimed her as his woman.

He didn't seem particularly thrilled about it, which made it difficult to accept that he had meant to say he loved her--particularly since she had only just tried to cut his heart out and she hadn't known him more than a few hours.

Of course, quite obviously, he had known of her for quite some time.

Still, that only left the suggestion that she had, in fact, been made *for* him.

He was wrong, of course, but that didn't mean he didn't believe it.

She'd been avoiding thinking about what he'd said before.

He'd said she was carrying his child. She waited, expecting a flood of disgust, revulsion. It didn't surface. She wondered if it was because her mind simply refused to accept the possibility, or if the possibility wasn't completely revolting to her.

Was it possible?

With an effort, she began to carefully reconstruct the events of the past several months. She'd always hated the physical examinations the company required. She'd never really known why because the truth was she never remembered anything that had happened--very little, anyway. She remembered undressing and lying on the examination table and staring up at the white lights above her head. Then, almost as if she blinked and it was over, or fell asleep, the tech would be telling her that she could get dressed and leave.

She knew it wasn't sleep, though. She couldn't recall the sensation of falling asleep. She couldn't recall any sense of sluggishness when she became aware again. It was more like a switch had been turned off--then turned on again.

Nausea washed over her.

Twice now, she remembered, Reuel had suggested that she was just the same as he was, a cyborg. When she'd tried to seize his ship, he'd called her a rogue hunter, gone rogue. She knew that was what he'd meant when he'd said she was his Eve.

It wasn't possible. She *remembered* her childhood! She remembered her parents. She was named for her mother and her last name, Varner-Hoskins 570, VH570--it was typical now to combine the names of both parents. The 570 only referenced the order of their family in the name pool.

It was purely coincidental that it also suggested one generation beyond Reuel's designation, 469. If what he was suggesting had been true, she would have been CO570, not VH570 ... unless.

She couldn't accept it. Cyborgs had no past, no childhood memories, no parents and therefore no memory of parents. Such things could have easily been planted in her mind, she knew, and she would not be able to tell the difference, but there was no reason that she could see why it would have been done. Why make her believe she was human if she wasn't?

The company would not have done that. There would have been no incentive, nothing to gain by it and they never did anything unless there was something to be gained from it.

Supposing, however, that whomever it was that had designed Reuel and the others had not been able to refrain from seeing if he could take it one step closer?

That still seemed unlikely. She still didn't believe it, but she had to accept that it *was* possible.

It seemed equally unlikely that Reuel would be wrong, however. Cyborgs were as precise and meticulous about gathering and collating information as any of their predecessors.

Leaving that line of thought for the moment, she went back to the possibility of the life growing inside of her. This time, a definite sense of warmth washed over her.

She summoned the computer assist again, commanding it to analyze the fluids Reuel had deposited inside of her. The results confused her further. The seminal fluids were barren of life seed.

An odd sense of loss filled her. She didn't want to examine it, though, and thrust the emotion away, commanding the computer to analyze the life growing inside of her.

Within moments, it began to furnish her with the stats. Her first feeling was one of relief. She hadn't harmed it. It still lived, was growing ... within a bio-engineered womb.

Her heart seemed to trip over itself. "Why is the womb bio-engineered, not natural?"

Insufficient data to determine.

"Was it transplanted to replace a defective organ?"

Negative.

"When was it implanted ... the womb?"

February fourteen twenty two hundred.

"That can't be right. That was on my birthday--three years ago. I'd remember that."

Date of activation.

"I was born--twenty years ago! I wasn't activated, you stupid, defective computer!"

Not surprisingly, the computer didn't respond.

"Give me the DNA of the life-form," Dalia said after a moment.

Combined DNA of donors Reuel, Cyborg Organism generation 479 and Dalia, Virtual Human generation 570. Donors each provided precisely half the combined DNA.

Dalia felt a sob of denial tear its way up her throat as the computer recited the codes. "What is the designation of the life-form?" she managed finally.

Unknown life-form.

Chapter Nine

Dalia felt numb, but the thought had no more than occurred to her than a hysterical urge to laugh assailed her. How could she *feel* anything? She wasn't human. Machines mimicked human emotions. They didn't, truly, feel them.

But she did. And Reuel did. And from what she could see, the others did.

It wasn't right that those bastards had allowed her to believe--no, *made* her believe--that she was human when she wasn't. Even worse, they had designed, programmed and trained her to kill her own kind--whatever that was.

What Reuel had done was just as wrong. She should hate him as much as she did the others who'd used her.

She wondered why she didn't.

Now that she knew everything--or much of it anyway--she couldn't help but wonder if he'd reprogrammed her mind *not* to hate him and the others. If he could infiltrate the company and impregnate her, that shouldn't have been beyond his capabilities.

She was going to go insane wondering how much of her memories was real, and how much was pure lies. How much of what she felt were her feelings?

Several hours passed before Reuel returned. He stood in the door way for several moments, holding a tray of food, and finally entered. Setting the tray on his desk, he pulled a drawer out, extracted a key and removed the manacles. She rubbed her wrists, studying him. Finally, she got up and went into the head.

She glanced toward the door to the corridor when she came out, but there wasn't much point in bolting. She had nowhere to go.

"I brought the food for you," he said, his voice carefully neutral.

She wasn't particularly hungry, but then she hadn't eaten much at breakfast, and she'd expended a good deal of energy fighting him--and--afterwards. She took the tray and sat cross-legged in the middle of the bed with it. He frowned, obviously not terribly happy about the idea of crumbs in his bed. Suppressing the urge to smile, she pretended to ignore him and ate the meal he'd brought.

"Is there some particular reason why I wasn't told?" she asked after a few moments, more because she was uncomfortable with his scrutiny than because she expected to get a straight answer from him.

He was very good at *appearing* to be completely open and actually telling her nothing at all.

"By the company?"

"By any damn body!" she retorted tightly.

He frowned, his lips tightening at her tone. "I wouldn't have told you at all if I'd believed that, in time, you'd learn to accept us. Your ... contempt for us, hatred of us, runs too deep, however. I realized that you would always hate us unless you could be brought to see that we are the same."

Dalia studied him a long moment and looked down at her food again. "Not as deep as you seem to think," she muttered. "If it did, I wouldn't have--done what I did a little while ago."

To her surprise, he colored faintly. "You were bound. I'm well aware I gave you no choice."

She shrugged. He was a real dolt if he thought she hadn't gone a good bit beyond submitting--or the call of duty for that matter. Maybe he'd been too enthralled to realize she was thoroughly enjoying it? Or, maybe, he thought she'd only pretended to enjoy it to get him to let his guard down?

The last seemed most likely.

"I won't apologize."

Dalia bit her lip, tamping the urge to smile, then concentrated on her food once more. "I'd be disappointed if you did," she murmured, "but you still didn't answer my question."

Something flickered across his face, but it was gone too quickly for her to grasp it. Relief?

He frowned. "I am Reuel CO469, prototype for those," he gestured toward the other end of the ship, "for all the CO469s. I was designed using the company's combined knowledge about robotics, bioengineering, artificial intelligence--even DNA structuring. When I was completed, they realized that I was more human than cyborg, which I have to suppose was the goal to start with. I had most of the advantages of being both, and few of the disadvantages--to their way of thinking, anyway. The problem arose that we knew we were cyborg. We were activated with that knowledge, with everything we needed to learn to become more human than cyborg, but none of the learning experiences necessary for humans to develop the correct emotional responses to given situations.

"Some of us managed to develop, more or less, normal responses anyway. Some did not and some simply could not accept that they weren't human and never could be. They developed abnormal emotional behavior and became dangerously unstable.

"The company had already embraced the CO469 enthusiastically, however. They'd produced nearly ten thousand before they discovered the design flaw."

Dalia almost choked on the drink of water she'd just taken. "Ten thousand! We were told there was less than a thousand!"

"You, of all people, are surprised that the company lied to you?" he murmured wryly. "They destroyed several thousand before they had ever been activated, but the company cringed at the loss and finally decided to try something else. They reprogrammed some ... not very successfully. Those had to be destroyed, as well, and they'd already sent out nearly five thousand.

"They created a new prototype--you. They gave you--almost--everything that they had given to me, but they were cautious for once. The first VT570s were all female, and designed to be like their human counterparts, physically smaller and weaker than the male CO469s. They were also given a childhood--everything it took to support the fantasy they had created--and not told that they were not human.

Since these were successful, they also produced male VT570s. All of them were designed to be rogue hunters ... to track down and destroy the CO469s.

"The things they learned from creating you, they were able to use to perfect some of the CO469s, protecting at least a part of their investment. But those who'd become completely unstable were beyond repairing and those who were not able to learn true emotional response were also defective in such a way that they could not recoup their losses, so those are the rogues that were first targeted for destruction.

"Phase two was to round up the remaining rogues and reprogram them."

Dalia frowned thoughtfully as she finished her meal and returned the tray to the desk. "I wasn't told-- *We* weren't told because they were afraid it would reverse the benefits of the additional programming?"

He shrugged. "I cannot say for certain, but very likely. It had the added benefit, though, of making the VT570 despise the CO469, which in turn made them very aggressive in tracking and killing the CO469. If they had informed the VT570 at any time, they ran the risk of having even more rogues on their hands."

"But you decided it was worth the risk in telling me?"

"We had little to lose."

Her lips tightened. "I, on the other hand, had a great deal to lose."

"Your ignorance?"

"My sanity," she said tartly.

He looked her over. "I did not consider that a risk. You are ... far stronger than a human; physically, mentally, emotionally."

"There was no reason why you should. As you pointed out, you had nothing to lose," Dalia retorted sharply.

"I said we had little."

It sounded like splitting hairs to her, but she let it drop. "Why did you impregnate me?"

Something flickered in his eyes. "I did not. I would gladly give up all the years that remain to me if I could. The gift of life is the one thing I would value above all else, but it's also the one thing I was not given."

Dalia frowned, but her inboard computer had told her as much. Still, the fetus contained his DNA. "You infiltrated the company. You did something to me--without my knowledge or consent. Cloning?"

"I did have the company infiltrated, and I did have you watched and studied. Six months ago we discovered that you had begun to produce live ovum... The company discovered it only a few months after we did. That is why you were ordered to come in for more tests, monthly. I had someone placed, at first, only to make certain the company didn't decide you were too dangerous to them to live.

"We had not found this to be the case in any of the CO469, and had to assume it was only the VT570 who were, possibly, capable of reproducing. You were the only one we had the chance to study, however, and we decided to see what would happen if male DNA was introduced at the time you produced a viable ovum. The CO469 was to introduce it, and inform me if you reproduced. The first two attempts failed. The third did not. Beyond supplying you with my DNA, however, I did nothing more."

"If it wasn't cloning, then what was it?"

"Abiogenesis."

Dalia frowned. "I'm not familiar with this term."

"Life will find a way--theoretically, spontaneous generation from non-living matter. Strictly speaking, perhaps not, but basically, abiogenesis. The cells I supplied could not be kept alive indefinitely, and we could not chance sending more without risking exposure. In your case, your body extracted the DNA from my cells and combined them with your own to complete the cycle."

It was a lot to absorb at one time. *She* had made herself pregnant? Maybe her own body had instigated the chemical process, maybe it would have anyway--they would certainly never know now--but, just as certainly, she hadn't done it completely by herself. "So--when the company discovered this--thing--growing inside of me, they panicked, ordered me destroyed? Where the hell was your inside man when I was running for my life?"

His eyes glittered, his face contorting with anger. "*It* is not a 'thing'. It is a child--mine and yours--or mine if you've no taste, or instinct, for mothering. It is hope--a future--purpose for our kind."

She was a little surprised at his ferocity in defending something that was, when all was said and done, none of his damned business. It was in her body. It was living and growing because of her and it would not survive without her to provide it with the sustenance it needed to continue to grow and develop.

For that matter, he had a hell of a nerve implying that she might not have motherly instincts. She had conceived the child, hadn't she? And, from what he'd said, with damned little help from him. She was just as intelligent as he was. If he could figure it out, she certainly could. "I suppose you think you have fatherly instincts?" she snapped.

"I will learn," he said tightly.

Her eyes narrowed, but she realized it was pointless to argue the matter now, when neither of them even knew if it would mature, particularly since she was not currently in a situation where she could prevent him from doing just as he pleased. "You damned near missed your chance," she retorted. "If I hadn't awakened when I did, we'd both be dead now--me and the--child."

"The one who infiltrated was discovered a week before your last examination and destroyed. We came when we learned of it but discovered the company had already attempted to destroy you, as well. I didn't know, for certain, that you had been impregnated until you told me when you--arrived."

There was at least some satisfaction in that, but it irritated the hell out of her to realize that she'd not only been used and chased after like a dangerous animal, she'd also been herded and trapped like one.

She extended her wrists. Reuel stared at them for several moments and finally looked up at her face. "You refuse to accept ... us?"

His hesitancy caught her attention. She had the feeling that he'd intended to say something else. "Truthfully? I don't know how I feel right now beyond angry. As far as I can see, you are no better than they are."

He flushed, but only partly from anger. "You will at least admit that there was no other way for us? If I had approached you openly, you would not have listened to anything I had to say. You would not have allowed me to try to persuade you. You would have done as you had been trained to do. You would have tried to kill me and I would have been forced to kill you to protect myself, or take you prisoner."

"As you did."

"The situation was different. You came to me for help."

"Which allowed you to use me."

His lips tightened. "If you can see only black and white, and nothing in between...." He broke off; his expression spoke eloquently of frustration. "I took the only course open to me. If you cannot accept that ... if you cannot also learn to forgive, then you're not as human as I believed and there is no hope for us."

As much as she would've liked it to be otherwise, she not only saw his point, she discovered she wanted to forgive him and accept him. She still didn't trust him, however, and until and unless she came to, she wasn't about to simply accept everything he had told her. "There is certainly no doubt in my mind that you are *very* human if you can believe, only because I enjoyed sex with you, that I'm going to believe everything you tell me and fall into your arms like a--complete fool!" she said tartly. "Learning to accept and forgive implies that I will be given time to."

Something gleamed in his eyes. A smile tugged at the corners of his lips, proving to her beyond a shadow of doubt that he was far more man than cyborg, and she didn't have to search hard to figure out why he looked so pleased.

She gave him a look. "Not that I have any interest in repeating it," she lied nastily. "But it was an interesting ... experiment." She had the satisfaction of seeing the smug look vanish, but somehow it wasn't nearly as satisfying as she'd hoped it would be.

She didn't want to examine why, but the pang she felt wouldn't allow her to lie to herself. The truth was, she was ready to forgive him now, because she did feel a connection to him and empathy. Finding herself in pretty much the same situation was probably a part of it. Discovering that the life growing inside of her was a part of him, she thought, had something to do with it as well, but it was still more complicated even than that.

Some ... transformation had begun inside of her from the moment she'd met him, maybe even before she'd met him. Maybe what he'd said before was truer than even he realized. Maybe she really was his Eve. Maybe she'd been predisposed from conception to feel as if she belonged with him.

She didn't know. What she did know was that she cared far more about him than she logically should have. She looked down at her hands and finally lowered them. "I give you my word I won't do anything that could cause harm to come to my child."

Chapter Ten

Despite their tentative truce, Dalia was surprised when they arrived at the rebel camp only a little over a week later. She would not have thought that Reuel trusted her enough to take her to the camp. She certainly would never have guessed that it was as close, relatively speaking, as it was.

Contrary to frequent speculation on the part of the company, the planet the rebels had chosen was well within the inner quadrant of settled worlds and, since they were more human, physiologically than droid, they had of necessity chosen one inhabitable by, and inhabited by, humans. It was a young planet, however, and far too primal to appeal to the more civilized tastes of the confederation. Only a few small colonies had been established there by members of the confederation and those were near the poles, where the temperature was somewhat cooler. The species of humans indigenous to the planet had not even reached the point in development where they had begun to form a recognizable societal structure.

Reuel had been carefully distant and polite since their confrontation, but he'd begun to pace the cabin he shared with her like a caged beast most nights instead of sharing the bed with her.

She supposed her nasty remark had convinced him any further attempts toward intimacy would be rebuffed. His guess wouldn't have been far off, not at first anyway.

She didn't trust him, and she knew she couldn't trust her own judgment if she allowed him to get too close. She needed time to decide whether she could accept what he'd done and why he'd done it. She needed time to accept the fact that her entire world as she'd known it had vanished. In the blink of an eye, she'd lost her past and her future. She'd lost herself--everything she'd ever believed was true, everything she'd ever believed in.

She thought she should have felt different, knowing now that she was not human. She couldn't decided whether the fact that she didn't meant that she hadn't fully grasped and accepted it, or if it meant that she *had* fully grasped and accepted it, and it didn't make as much difference to her as she would've thought it would have.

One thing that did not change was her desire for Reuel. She'd found him attractive the moment she saw him. Being with him had only increased her attraction to him because it had ceased to be a matter of thinking he appealed to her and become an absolute certainty the moment he touched her intimately.

Unfortunately, by the time she'd come around to the realization that there was no sense in depriving herself of enjoying his caresses, they had arrived on the rebel world and Reuel, showing every sign of relief, had escaped her clutches.

Dalia was in the cabin when they landed. Reuel had given her permission to roam the ship at will once more, but she wasn't comfortable with the brooding, speculative looks the men cast at her. She supposed she had no right to quibble. She might not have instigated the little erotic scene in the rec room, but she had made no attempt to stop it either. The truth was, despite the fact that she'd never engaged in sexual activities before, she was neither self-conscious nor in any way inhibited about sexuality. It would never have occurred to her to engage in any sort of sexual act publicly, but she'd found it wildly stimulating. Most of it had simply been Reuel, but she couldn't deny, to herself at least, that being watched and desired had added a touch of spice to it.

If it had disturbed anyone, it was Reuel. She had the distinct feeling that he not only regretted yielding to whatever demon had prompted him to do it because he thought it had angered and distressed her, but also that it irked him that he'd 'shared' her sexually. He'd developed the habit since of staring darkly at any of the men who looked at her as if he needed only a nudge of provocation to tear their heads off.

There was a hesitancy about his attitude as he stood in the doorway of the cabin studying her, that it sent a wave of uneasiness through her. When she turned to look at him, she saw he was holding a pair of manacles. "You are a prisoner of the Cyborg Liberation. I cannot allow you to roam freely when we leave the ship."

Dalia stared at him in disbelief. "You're not serious!"

"I am."

"Exactly what is it that you suspect that I will do?"

"Leave--at the very first opportunity."

Dalia didn't deny it. Truthfully, she was a little surprised he hadn't accused her of having thoughts about sabotage. As far as escaping went, she hadn't considered it, mostly because she hadn't expected him to bring her to the rebel stronghold. She knew there was a better than even chance that she *would* have thought of it at some point, however. She knew she wouldn't be accepted by the other rogues-- rebels--certainly not at first, anyway. From what she could tell, Reuel was their leader, and she knew he would protect the child she carried, whatever he thought of her. Unless he chained her to his wrist, though, she was bound to have some unpleasant, potentially dangerous, confrontations and it was possible she'd find this no healthier an atmosphere for her continued existence than being in the bosom of the company.

Even though she hadn't spent a lot of time thinking about what she would do beyond escaping the company's assassins, she certainly hadn't had any desire or intention of joining those she'd spent the past several years tracking.

She had to suppose Reuel was well aware that she hadn't resigned herself to accept what he thought she couldn't change.

Glaring at him, she held out her wrists for the restraints. Without a word, he secured the manacles to her wrists, then led her down the companionway to the cockpit. The four who'd traveled with them were already strapped in for landing. Guiding her to the first seat they came to, he strapped her in before moving to the console to land the craft.

As resentful as she was about being relegated to the status of secured prisoner once more, she quickly discovered strapping her into her seat wasn't just an extension of her loss of privilege. The moment the craft dropped through the planet's atmosphere, it was bounced around like a leaf caught in a vortex. She clamped her teeth together to keep from biting her tongue, closing her eyes as the craft shimmied so hard it rattled even her eyes in her head, making her see double. For perhaps ten minutes, the shaking grew progressively worse until she'd begun to wonder if the craft would still be sound enough to land. Finally, the shaking and bouncing began to taper off.

When she opened her eyes again, she could see that they'd dropped low enough the green below them was beginning to take the shape of individual trees. The green gave way to devastation--brown and blackened trees, scorched earth and flowing, red streams, and, in the center of it, she saw the smoking top of a volcano that looked to be about as tall as a hundred story building. They passed over a smaller one before landmass gave way to sea. In the distance, another landmass emerged from the mist and the sea, looking, at first, like nothing more than a dark cloud hovering on the horizon.

As they neared it, she could see that it wasn't a single landmass, but islands, pushed up from the sea by volcanic activity so long ago that a young forest covered the crown of several of them. Bald red cliffs rose from the sea perhaps a hundred feet almost vertically on the largest of the islands, the one she saw that they were headed for.

The craft dropped lower as they neared, coming in uncomfortably close to the tops of the trees. The altitude prevented her from seeing the stockade until they were upon it. The moment they cleared the outer wall, the craft dropped to the ground and settled with a bone-jarring, teeth-rattling finality that made Dalia wonder for several seconds if they'd crashed, a confusion compounded by the fact that they'd scarcely come to a complete halt when the men threw off their restraints, jumped to their feet, and stampeded toward the gangplank as if the ship would explode any moment.

She relaxed fractionally when Reuel, looking completely unruffled and unhurried, sauntered back to where she was seated and unfastened her. Helping her to her feet, he herded her before him.

She didn't know what she'd expected, but what she saw wasn't it. Surrounding the camp was a stockade that appeared to have been made out of trees that had been stripped of their limbs, leaves, and bark, and then driven into the ground. The compound itself was dotted with stumps, some level with the dirt, others protruding from it anywhere from two to five feet. A small waterfall had been encompassed by the stockade at one end. A pool formed at its base, then meandered across the compound, forming a shallow brook. Scattered about the compound in no sort of order that she could discern were crude shelters, also constructed of raw timber and roofed, from what she could see, with the limbs that had been shaved from the trees.

She'd seen primitive villages over the years, but this stunned her. Reuel gave her a nudge, breaking through her shocked dismay, and she made her way down the gangplank. The ground, she quickly discovered, was littered with rocks and debris like a minefield. She watched her feet as Reuel grasped her arm and led her through the crude village. She tried to avoid as much as she could, but walking was painful. After a moment, Reuel scooped her into his arms and carried her, and she was able to look around once more.

Most of the structures they passed were only partially constructed--she assumed they were, at any rate. They were little more than posts with a thatch of limbs supported between them. She saw maybe a dozen inhabitants moving about, but only a few of them appeared to be engaged in any task.

Reuel took her to the largest, complete structure near where they'd landed and set her on her feet once more when they were inside. It was as crude inside as out, and contained very little. The room he led her to had no window, and certainly no artificial light, but it wasn't really necessary. There was enough light pouring through the roof and walls to fully illuminate the small space, which contained nothing more than a narrow cot, a crude table and chair that looked as if they'd been made of unrefined wood, a large container she saw held water and a smaller, empty one, that she simply stared at for several moments as the revolting realization slowly filtered into her mind that it was meant for use when it was necessary to eliminate her body waste.

She realized Reuel had released her arm at the doorway and turned to look at him.

"What now?"

"We wait."

With that, he stepped out, closed the door, and bolted it with a heavy chain.

She stared at the chain, then peered at Reuel's retreating form through the gaps between the wood as he left the hut and finally disappeared completely from view. Still feeling strangely blank, she moved to the cot, tested it to make sure it wouldn't collapse when she put her weight on it, and finally sat. "Wait for what?" she muttered.

She frowned thoughtfully, studying the room around her. She wasn't accustomed to luxury by any means, but she was used to far more civilized surroundings. Was this ... crude, purely utilitarian, and not very functional at that, village the result of life on the move? Because the rebels were mostly male and didn't care a great deal about comfort? Or was there another explanation for this ... atrocity that didn't immediately present itself?

The entire place looked as if it had been thrown together hastily. In fact, now that she thought about it, everything looked so raw she knew it couldn't possibly even have been here more than a few weeks at the outside. Despite the half finished structures they'd passed, it also didn't look like a place that had been planned for permanence. For, surely, if it had been, they would have taken the time to build more sturdy shelters?

She shook her head. The whole situation was just so completely bizarre she couldn't get her mind around it. Finally, she got off the cot and went to peer through the cracks in the wall. She'd checked the entire circumference of the outer wall of the structure before she realized that she couldn't see anything at all from her jail cell. She could *hear* activity, but it was hard to tell what they were doing. Hours passed. Occasionally, she would hear someone pass close by and she would jump up and move to the wall to watch them until they disappeared from view, but otherwise, she had nothing to occupy her but the puzzle she was trying to piece together.

Toward evening, when the sun had sunk low enough that the light had begun to dim in the room, Reuel returned with food. To her surprise, instead of leaving once he'd handed it to her, he moved around the room outside her cell restlessly while she ate. Deciding he must be waiting to take the tray with him, she moved to the door and shoved it under once she'd finished. Instead of taking it and leaving, however, he set it aside, opened the door again, and tossed a pair of boots to her.

"Put these on."

Surprised, she stared at him a couple of minutes and finally pulled the boots on. They fit as if they'd been made for her, and she assumed they must have been. They'd been fashioned out of something that looked like skin, animal skin she assumed from the thickness. It made her feel a little queasy to think she'd thrust her feet into something that had once been living, but it seemed par for the situation. They didn't appear to have any facilities for making things out of synthetic materials, or making synthetic material for that matter.

Catching her arm, he led her from the structure in the direction of the waterfall. She saw he was carrying a small bundle under his arm, but she didn't question it until they reached the pool. Settling the bundle on a stump jutting from the ground, he opened it and handed her something that looked like a rock.

"Soap--washcloth," he said succinctly. "Bathe."

She stared at him and then looked around. "In that?" she asked in dismay, pointing toward the pool. "But--it'll contaminate the water!"

For the first time since he'd come to the cabin on the ship earlier, a smile tugged at his lips. "We get our drinking water from a well."

Dalia didn't feel an answering amusement. She looked at the pool of water again. "Aren't there--living things in it?"

"They won't bother you."

It wasn't the answer she'd wanted. A simple 'no' would have made her feel worlds better.

This, she supposed, explained Reuel's penchant for antiquated things--like water in the particle bath. "What if the water covers my head?" she said uneasily.

"Hold your breath."

"I'm so glad you find this amusing!" she said tartly.

He chuckled. "The pool is only a few feet deep. You won't be submerged unless you fall down. If you fall, get up."

Smart ass, Dalia thought irritably as she sat down and tugged the boots off. When she stood once more, she looked down at the tunic she was wearing--another of those Reuel had supplied for her to wear. With her wrists manacled, she couldn't take it off. Since he hadn't offered to unlock the manacles, she assumed she was expected to bathe in it. Mentally shrugging, she turned to study the water again. The bank sloped down to the water's surface, but not steeply. She thought she could manage to walk down it without slipping.

Reuel caught hold of the tunic as she took a step toward it. "You need to take this off."

She turned and gave him a look. "My wrists are manacled together. Just how do you propose I do that?"

He frowned and patted the pockets of his trousers. His lips twisted wryly and she knew he hadn't brought the key.

It seemed unlikely that he'd 'forgotten'. Cyborgs didn't have 'memory lapses'. They might fail to observe. They might be deactivated, making it impossible to record. They might even suffer outside interference of their recording abilities, but they didn't 'forget'.

On the other hand, he'd brought the bundle when he'd brought her meal. Bringing her down to bathe certainly wasn't an impulse.

Whatever it was he'd been doing since they'd arrived had undoubtedly so completely absorbed his attention that he'd overlooked that one important detail.

She was still wondering what could possibly have required so much of his active mental resources when he grasped the shoulders of the tunic and separated the seams. The tunic fell to her feet. She stared down at it with a combination of surprise and dawning outrage. "Your disregard for husbanding your resources borders on criminal!" she snapped angrily.

"It's my tunic," he pointed out. "And I'm already a criminal. What will they do? Jail me first for ten years, then execute me?"

"But I was wearing it!"

"I broke the seams. It's repairable."

That seemed inarguable, but she was still irritated. Without another word, she turned and made her way to the pool. She hesitated at the edge and finally stepped in. To her surprise, the water was warm, almost hot in fact. After a fractional hesitation, she placed her other foot into the water and moved away from the edge until the water was lapping her knees.

Despite his reassurances, she didn't want to test whether or not it got any deeper. Bending at the waist, she wet the cloth. Something drew her attention as she did so, and as she straightened once more, she glanced around at Reuel.

He was standing where she'd left him, staring at her, or rather her ass, as if every brain function had shut down. Apparently her stillness filtered through, for after several moments, he blinked. When he did, she turned around once more, frowning thoughtfully as she lathered the cloth in her hand.

After a moment, a faint smile curled her lips as the realization settled in upon her that, regardless of what he thought of her or felt toward her, he still desired her.

She didn't consciously set out to seduce him. She didn't even actually consider teasing him. To begin with, it was more a matter of curiosity than anything else that spurred her to experiment to see what she might do that would have a similar effect on him.

Dropping the soap, she bent at the waist once more and lathered her thighs with slow deliberation. When she twisted around to rub the cloth over her buttocks, she saw that he had that glassy-eyed look of complete absorption again, watching as she rubbed the cloth slowly over first one buttock and then the other and finally slipped the cloth along the cleft between the two.

He blinked when she did that, swallowing as if it took an effort to gather enough moisture into his mouth to complete the action. Warmth spread through her as she watched his face and she lost track of why she'd begun the tease him in the first place.

Straightening once more, she turned to face him as she rubbed the cloth over her breasts, down her belly and between her legs. He studied her hand for several moments before his gaze lifted to meet hers.

For several moments, neither of them so much as breathed. Abruptly, he strode toward her.

Chapter Eleven

Dalia felt her heart execute an erratic little stammer and then begin to race, as if struggling to regain its rhythm. Adrenaline gushed into her system, bringing a flush of hypersensitivity to her skin as Reuel reached her. Without hesitation, he wrapped his arms around her and pulled her flush against him, lifting her up to meet him as he lowered his head and covered her mouth with his own.

A deep sense of gratification filled her as he flooded her senses with himself. She had wanted him, but she hadn't realized how deeply she had hungered for his caresses until she felt it gnawing at her vitals, felt her body clamor with instant need as her mind and body absorbed his scent and taste as if his essence were as essential to her as air and water.

A jolt went through him as he felt the chain of the manacle glide up his chest as she reached upward to grip his shoulders. Breaking the kiss, he straightened, lifting her off her feet and guiding her legs around his waist. She locked her ankles behind his back and lifted her arms, looping them around his shoulders and spearing her fingers through his dark hair as she lifted her lips to his once more.

He seized upon her offering like a starving man, his mouth hungry and demanding and supplicating all at once as he delved his tongue into her mouth and rubbed it sensuously, possessively along the tender inner flesh of her mouth, sending a flood of heat through her. Sharp needles of sensation wove through her, absorbed into her flesh at every point she brushed against him despite the teasing barrier his clothing presented.

Frustrated, she grasped the fabric of his tunic and gathered it into her fists, tugging it upward. He helped her, shrugging his arms from it, breaking the kiss long enough to pull it over his head and toss it in the direction of the bank before he hoisted her higher and kissed her throat and the upper slope of her breasts.

Moisture flooded her sex in a wash of anticipation as she felt him fumbling at his trousers. But the moment his mouth moved downward and covered the aching tip of one breast, her entire world focused on that one point of intensely delightful sensation. She gasped. Her arms tightened around his head, clutching him to her.

He had aligned his body with hers and thrust upward, pushing down on her hips at the same time and sinking the head of his cock inside of her before she realized he meant to enter her. A whimper of pleasure escaped her and he lifted his head, his gaze locking with hers as he bore her hips inexorably downward until she was impaled to the hilt of his cock. She panted as she felt her body stretching, adjusting to his hard, unyielding flesh, but the sensations palpitating through her were so exquisite she found it impossible to remain still. She moved restlessly against him, urging him to move inside of her.

His face went taut, twisted as her movements drove him over the edge. Gripping her hips almost bruisingly, he lifted her up and pushed her down again, sheathing himself inside her, withdrawing, and pushing again in rough, jerky motions that drove her into mindless ecstasy. Within moments, she felt herself hovering on the brink and then pitching over it into blissful oblivion as pleasure rocked her body. Almost simultaneously, as if her own culmination had pushed him over the edge as well, she felt his body convulsing in completion, felt the jerk of his cock as his release exploded from him in a crescendo of passion.

His arms tightened around her as Dalia felt her own body go limp with relief. He swayed slightly. With an effort, Dalia lifted her arms from around his neck, gripping his shoulders. Withdrawing his spent flesh from her body, he allowed her to slide slowly down his length until her feet touched the ground. He pulled her close once more, running a hand caressingly along her back, but she sensed that he'd withdrawn, distancing himself from her emotionally.

Discomfort settled over her, making her feel suddenly awkward. She wondered how it was that they could meld so completely, pleasure each other so thoroughly, and still feel such distrust of one another that they could find no common ground on a mental or emotional level.

This was the point, in the afterglow of their pleasure, where they should be expressing deeper feelings--or polite thank yous for a good fuck at the very least, but she couldn't express what she didn't understand and she couldn't bring herself to denigrate what happened between them by acting as if he'd just handed her a bouquet of flowers. Clearing her throat uncomfortably, she pushed against him. When he released her, she turned away without meeting his eyes and looked around for the soap he'd given her.

She saw it had floated halfway across the pool and, with a sense of relief that she had something to do besides stand around and avoid his gaze, she went after it.

He stood where she'd left him, studying her while he absently removed the rest of his clothing and began to bathe himself, waiting, she sensed, for her to say something. Instead of diminishing, the sense of awkwardness intensified as she finished her bath. What did he expect her to say? Its a damn shame we're enemies, because I really enjoy having sex with you? I wish you'd considered wooing me before you fucked me over?

She considered herself a reasonable person. Under the circumstances, she couldn't really fault him for the course he'd taken. He'd had no reason to believe she would be anything but hostile and uncooperative. The truth was, she probably would have been.

So what did that mean? There never would have been a chance for them, no matter what?

She frowned at that thought, wondering, if she really did consider him an enemy, and if she really did distrust and despise him for what he'd done, why she would think it at all.

The answer was simple, but not something she felt like she could accept.

She had to consider that her logic must be faulty at present. If she accepted everything that he'd told her, then her body was in the grips of some hormonal and chemical changes that she'd never before experienced. It stood to reason those changes would affect her logical brain functions.

She could not trust her judgment, not when she knew that Reuel was a dangerous, and, from what she knew from personal experience, ruthless, man.

Shaking off her thoughts, she finished her bath, climbed from the pool, and dried herself off with the length of cloth Reuel had brought for that purpose. After a moment, Reuel followed suit, collected the clothing he'd tossed onto the bank, and began tugging his clothes on once more. When she'd finished drying off, she wrapped the cloth around her since she couldn't dress with the manacles attached to her wrists.

Reuel looked displeased, but it was hardly her fault. If he didn't want her parading around the compound half naked, he should have remembered to bring the key or not manacled her to begin with.

She supposed she could see his point to an extent. Despite the nearly twenty-foot stockade that encompassed the perimeter of the compound, it didn't look very secure. If she'd had the desire to escape, there wouldn't have been much to even slow her down. She could jump a good fifteen feet flat footed, so the stockade itself was no hindrance. Besides, she suspected there would have to be large gaps in the stockade on each end where it crossed the water. She could see the water was flowing freely. She still had no idea of how many Cyborg inhabited this camp, but there were certainly not many--too few to present much of a problem if she'd decided to sneak out after dark.

Dismissing her irritation, she tugged her boots on, tucked her towel snugly around her breasts, and headed back. Reuel caught up to her after only a few steps, catching hold of her upper arm.

It was almost dark by the time they reached the structure where she was being held. Inside, it was completely dark.

Reuel pulled her to a halt on the threshold and moved inside. After a few moments of listening to furtive movements and wondering what he was about, her curiosity was appeased when light blossomed around them, illuminating the interior of the structure. She saw Reuel was holding a small, cuplike object. Whatever it was inside the container was on fire. She shouldn't have been surprised considering the crudeness of everything else she'd seen since she'd arrived, but open flame for lighting in a structure made entirely of drying wood seemed foolhardy to say the least and she wondered if the Cyborgs had escaped with little more than the clothing on their backs.

That thought brought her back to the puzzle the entire situation represented to her mind and she wondered again why it was that this place felt so wrong. In a way, she supposed, it did make sense. The Cyborgs were on the run and had been since they'd gone rogue. They had certainly not had time to establish a place of permanence. It also made sense that if they had to move frequently for security reasons that they would not attempt to acquire a great deal.

She supposed what made her feel the 'wrongness' of it was that Reuel simply didn't behave at all like someone on the run. He was cautious, alert, prepared, but completely cool and collected as if he knew exactly what to expect and was prepared for it. There was no evidence of nervousness or fear in Reuel, or any of the others for that matter. If he'd been no more than what the company claimed the Cyborgs to be, emotionless machines incapable of anything more than mimicking the emotions of the humans they emulated, she wouldn't have questioned it. She knew better, though. She knew Reuel was capable of feeling the full spectrum, just as she, who'd believed she was human, could feel them.

It coalesced in her mind that that was exactly what made this situation feel wrong. The compound looked thrown together. It looked like something one would expect to see if one were looking for a group that was fighting a running battle. The truth was the cyborgs didn't behave as if they were engaged in a fight and flight campaign.

Still puzzling over it, Dalia went into the cell, discarded the cloth and settled on the bunk, tugging the boots off. She doubted Reuel would leave the light, just in case she took the notion of burning the place down to escape, and, in any case, she found she was tired enough to rest. To her surprise, Reuel followed her inside and set the light down.

Surprise gave way to something else, however, as he coolly began to remove his clothes. Despite the fact that he'd thoroughly pleasured her only a little while earlier, anticipation filtered through her mind. A prick of irritation surfaced, as well, that he seemed to expect her to welcome his sexual advances. But then she certainly hadn't given him any reason to think otherwise and the truth was, she did. She saw no reason to pretend that she didn't at this point.

Settling back on the bed, she propped her arms behind her head and watched the flickering light lick over him in a wash of golden light, completely enthralled by the bunching and flexing of his muscles as he tugged the tunic over his head and tossed it aside. His boots, still wet from wading into the pool, proved difficult. He sat down on the edge of the cot and tugged them off, then stood once more and shucked his trousers.

His member was fully erect when he pushed his trousers down his hips, rising almost vertically from the nest of dark hair low on his belly. Dalia stared at it, feeling the sense of excitement rise as memories flickered through her mind with a rush of heat.

Without hesitation, she reached for him when he'd stepped out of his trousers. The taut look left his face. Placing one knee between her parted thighs, he covered her body with his own, kissing her with the ravenousness of a man dying of hunger, as if the bout of love making at the pool had done no more than whet his appetite. It was almost disconcerting, but far more comforting than unnerving to find she had such an effect on him, for she could not deny that each encounter left her hungering for more.

And, despite the urgency she sensed in him, he made no effort to penetrate her body at once. Instead, he roamed her flesh with his hands, his lips, and his tongue, endlessly it seemed. He coaxed heated desire from her and then stoked it higher and higher with each attentive caress until she was writhing beneath him in an agony of need. She began to beg him to fill her, to bring her to fulfillment, with moans, throaty whimpers of need, arching against him.

He remained deaf to her subtle pleas, pushing her thighs wide and stroking one long finger along her cleft, rubbing it round and round her clit as he sucked first one nipple and then the other until she began to struggle against him, digging her nails into the flesh of his shoulders. She gasped his name, desperation in her voice, began to chant it as she felt the tension building inside of her until she knew she would climax without him ever having fully claimed her body. She fought it, struggling to keep it at bay until she could feel his cock stroking the tender flesh inside of her.

Abruptly, his own restraint broke and he rose on his knees. Catching her ankles, he jerked her hips free of the bed and, holding her legs against his chest, aligned his body with hers and rammed into her in one hard thrust, impaling her with his cock as if he had stabbed her. His possession caught her by surprise, forced the air from her lungs in a rush, and tore her resistance from her grasp. The inner walls of her sex quaked with shocked delight as he pulled a little way out and thrust again, in a short, hard ramming motion that sent her over the edge so suddenly that a strangled scream was torn from her.

Releasing her legs, he tumbled on top of her, scooping her into a tight embrace and covered her mouth in a deep kiss that seemed in direct opposition to his possession of her body as he continued thrusting inside of her in hard, sharp thrusts as if he were intent on stabbing her to death.

She felt as if she were dying--of pleasure too intense to contain, felt blackness creep in around her as her body continued to shudder and convulse in release. He wrenched his mouth from hers and released a growl of satisfaction as his body abruptly answered the call of hers and yielded him up to his own release. Shuddering, he half collapsed on top of her, struggling to catch his breath. After a moment, he gathered himself and rolled off of her onto the bed beside her. To her surprise, he took her with him, tucking her tightly against his side as if he would never let her go.

For the first time since she'd met him, she accepted the feeling unquestioningly, accepted the curious warmth and sense of peace that flowed through her as she settled against him and gave herself up to the urge to slip away from consciousness.

She slept so deeply, she hardly stirred when he moved away from her in the predawn, dressed and left her in soul possession of her cell. A sense of well-being filled her when she rose finally ... a sense that lasted until her noon meal was delivered by a female cyborg.

Although she said nothing, the woman was openly hostile. After doing nothing more than plunking a tray of food inside the door, she slammed it shut again, locked it, tugged on the chain a couple of times to make certain it would hold, and then left again without once uttering a word.

It was Dalia's first real taste of being a prisoner among them. Reuel, she realized, had been angry with her and distrustful, but he had also given her the sense, from the very first, that he felt she belonged with them, that he wanted to accept her.

She wondered if the woman represented the general feelings toward her, or if she had a personal reason for being so hostile. That thought brought others that were not welcome and left her with a vague sense of uneasiness and anger.

Boredom chased both away as the day wore on, however. As she had the day before, she spent most of her time pacing and peering through the crevices between the upright posts, trying to figure out what was happening. She could see nothing and she began to wonder if this was to be her routine and how long they, or rather Reuel, would consider it necessary to keep her under lock and key.

She was fairly certain the boredom would drive her mad if it continued long. She was accustomed to being active. Being imprisoned, with nothing to occupy her but her doubts and fears began to weigh upon her before she'd spent her second day in the small cell.

On the third day, however, all hell broke loose.

Chapter Twelve

"If you only meant to hold me prisoner I can't imagine why you even bothered to bring me here," Dalia said coldly when Reuel arrived with her evening meal as he had the day before. She'd been hopeful of seeing him all day long but as the day wore on and boredom set in, irritation with him had set in, as well.

He studied her a long moment before he moved across the room and set the tray he was carrying down. "I told you why we brought you."

Her lips tightened. "Only to see if I can produce a living being? What then? What if it's just some horrible, malformed creature? It isn't human. The computer cannot identify it and therefore cannot ascertain the 'normality' of it.

"You implied ... more," she finished with a touch of petulance.

"You are carrying the child of a new race of beings. The computer cannot be expected to analyze it with no data, but there is no reason to believe that it isn't perfectly healthy and normal ... for a cyborg. Is that why you're angry? You're afraid for the child?"

Instead of answering, she looked away from him, realizing he was right. She was afraid. She'd been too shocked when she'd first learned of it to absorb that she was to become a mother. But her belly, once concave when she lay flat, had filled in, and then had begun to round outward with its growth, making it impossible to ignore even if she'd wanted to once she'd realized what the change meant. In any case, since she'd learned of it, she'd had far too much time to do nothing but think. She'd not only begun to feel a tentative pleasure in the idea, she'd also begun to wonder about the tiny being growing inside of her and to worry that something would go wrong.

Taking her silence as an affirmation, he moved toward her, kneeling beside the bed where she sat. "Nature has seen fit to intervene on our behalf. Even though our creators had no mercy upon us, or empathy for what they had done in creating us and then leaving us in limbo, neither human nor machine, nature has taken us the next step in evolution, made us beings in our own right.

"It's something to rejoice in, not fear. I'm as certain of it as I have ever been of anything."

Dalia looked at him doubtfully. "Nature has produced as many disasters as man. Even man no longer trusts his destiny entirely to the whims of nature. How safe are we to do so?"

He studied her for several moments and finally moved to sit on the cot next to her, pulling her onto his lap. "In the beginning, I had no goal in mind, no plan for a future I couldn't even conceive. I left only because I couldn't bear to be among humans and not be accepted as one, because I wanted the right to make my own choices, to make my own life. I hated them then, but I feel no animosity toward them now. All I want is freedom, and peace to build my own world, with my own people.

"I am ... as afraid as you are that something will go wrong, but it's not because I expect it will so much as it's because I want it so much."

Dalia stiffened when Reuel pulled her onto his lap, not the least because she wasn't ready to forgive him for ignoring her all day. She found, though, that there was a seductive quality to being held in such a way that had nothing to do with sexual arousal, but everything to do with feeling as if one belonged. Slowly, as his voice washed over her, she relaxed. "And now? What is it that you plan to do?"

He hesitated. "Wait."

"For the birth of the child?"

"Among other things."

And what then, she wondered? Would he have no further use for her? Would he simply discard her? "Human gestation takes between nine and ten months, almost a year. Unless the rapid cell regeneration that makes us heal faster also effects the growth of the child, that could be ... many more months. You'll keep me prisoner till then?"

Again, he hesitated. "Until my heart tells me that you accept ... or that you will never accept."

"What is it that you want, truly?"

Hooking a finger under her chin, he nudged her face up and kissed her lightly, then scooped her from his lap, dropped her onto the bed, and handed her the tray of food.

"Eat."

She picked up her fork and began to eat. "You're not going to answer that, are you?"

He scrubbed his hands over his face. "Honestly? I don't want to think about it. Not now. Not when things are still so uncertain."

She allowed the subject to drop, certain she could dig no more out of him. As before, he'd hinted that there could be much more for them, but he refused to be pinned down.

In any case, it occurred to her presently that they would probably go down to the pool to bathe as they had the night before and her appetite for food vanished. He didn't disappoint her--on any level.

When she'd finished and set the tray aside, he rose and escorted her to the pool. Unlike the night before, however, he removed the manacles and, as she undressed, he stripped his own clothing off. Anticipation tightened in her belly as she moved down to the pool with her bathing supplies.

She quickly discovered, however, that Reuel was anything but predictable. She'd no sooner stepped gingerly into the edge of the pool than he sailed past her, landing in the middle of the pool so hard he created a twenty-foot blast radius of displaced water, drenching her abruptly from head to toe. Gasping from surprise, Dalia pushed the soaked hair from her eyes and whirled to look at him.

He was floating on his back, a grin of pure mischief lighting his eyes and his face in a way that made her heart stutter to a halt almost painfully in her chest. She felt an answering smile curl her own lips, despite her disappointment over the fact that he did not, apparently, intend to assault her--not sexually anyway. "You ...

asshole!" she said, half laughing, half in irritation. "I'm soaking wet!"

He didn't look the least put out by the insult. Instead, he chuckled. "That's the general idea when you bathe in water."

Glaring at him, she slapped the water with her hand, sending a light spray into his face. His grin vanished as he mopped the water from his face, but his eyes still gleamed with amusement. "This means war, woman," he growled, getting to his feet and advancing on her.

Dalia gaped at him for several moments before finally, with a shriek, she whirled to flee. He caught her around the waist, snatching her off her feet and spun with her in a tight circle that made her head swim. Her stomach went weightless. When he set her abruptly on her feet once more, she staggered dizzily and fell back against him, knocking him off balance. He landed on his butt, sending up another geyser of water, and Dalia landed on his lap.

She was laughing when she turned to look at him. "I haven't done that since I...." Her amusement vanished. A sense of terrible loss replaced it. "I've never done that, have I?"

Reuel's amusement died. His gaze flickered over her face searchingly. Finally, he cupped her face in his hands, carefully smoothing the wet tendrils of hair from her cheeks. "The memories you give our child will be real-- from now on, *all* of your memories will be yours."

Dalia nodded, finally, completely, understanding what he'd been trying to tell her for the past several weeks. He wasn't asking her to give up something she had for a dream that might never materialize. He was telling her she had never had it to begin with, that she couldn't lose what had never been hers, but she had a great deal to gain if she was strong enough and determined enough to reach for it.

Understanding didn't make the hurt go away, however, and she couldn't prevent tears from filling her eyes. She felt as if she'd just learned of the deaths of her parents all over again, the same wrenching pain of loss, even though she knew they had never been her parents at all. The memories of her happy childhood with them had buoyed her spirits even when she missed them. Now, she didn't even have that.

She had what Reuel had--nothing, only a moment of awakening.

Oddly enough, that realization dulled the hurt as nothing else. "You didn't even have the illusion."

He shrugged, withdrawing both physically and emotionally. "Illusions bring no comfort."

She watched him as he waded to the edge of the pool and gathered the soap and cloths, knowing he was wrong. Her mind might tell her that everything Reuel said about her programming was true, that nothing she believed she remembered had been real, but her heart still believed. Her heart would always believe as long as it remained in her memory, and she would draw sustenance from it.

Where had he found the strength to open his heart to feeling?

If she had awakened to the world that he had, she didn't think she could have handled it. She would have gone mad as, in fact, some of them had.

She was sorry to see his playfulness vanish. It was a side of him that she would never have expected. And, as handsome as he was to her at any time, he had never looked more handsome than when laughter lit his face. The urge to summon that carefree expression once more was strong, but she could think of nothing to do or say that might bring it to the surface once more.

Sighing, she finished her bath and climbed out to dry off. Reuel was so quick to follow her that she was left in no doubt that his trust in her was virtually nil, regardless of what had passed between them.

Up until that moment, she hadn't cared. It had exasperated her, but she'd accepted that it was warranted. It hadn't wounded her. She wasn't sure she wanted to know why it did now.

Without a word, she extended her arms for the manacles when they'd finished dressing. He seemed disinclined to talk, and she wasn't feeling particularly talkative herself.

She was certain she'd also lost all desire for sex, as well, until Reuel closed the door behind them, stripped, and proceeded to torment her until she was mindless with need and begging him to take her.

Apparently unconvinced that he'd thoroughly satisfied her, he made love to her twice more before they both dropped into the sleep of the truly sated and exhausted.

It was still dark when someone began banging on the door.

Reuel sat up abruptly. "What is it?"

"They're coming."

"Is everything ready?"

"I think ... yes. But, Reuel, they slipped in. I don't know how they managed it, but they're practically on top of us and ... there's about twice as many as we'd expected."

"Shit!"

Dalia sat up as Reuel leapt from the bed. "What is it?"

"The company." His face was grim as he lit the lamp and began snatching his cloths on.

"Oh my god! How? How could they have found us?"

Reuel turned and looked at her grimly.

A cold chill went through her. "I didn't! Reuel, I swear to you, it wasn't me! I cut my locator out and destroyed it. You've seen the scar!"

His lips tightened, but he shook his head. "You took one out."

She gaped at him. "But ... there was only one. I rememb...." A terrible fear seized her. She scrambled to her feet. "Please, Reuel. Believe me! I didn't knowingly bring them down on us."

He shook her off. "It doesn't matter now."

Dalia swallowed with an effort. "It matters to me."

His gaze flickered over her face. "I have to go."

The words were scarcely out of his mouth when an explosion of white light lit the world outside as if it were daylight. Almost instantly, an ear splitting concussion followed and directly behind that everything around them shuddered.

"Neutron," Dalia gasped, staring down at her hands, expecting them to disintegrate before her eyes.

When she looked up again, she saw Reuel's eyes were trained upon the ceiling, as if he could see through it. "The shield won't take many hits like that," he said grimly. Turning, he strode to the door.

Dalia stared at him, too stunned to assimilate what he'd just said. A shield?

He paused at the door and turned to look at her. Swallowing with an effort, he pulled the key from his pocket and tossed it to her. "Give me your word, Dalia. If this goes badly, don't let them take you. Don't give yourself up. There's a craft hidden in a cave north of here. Take it and find a safe place to raise our child."

Dalia blinked at him uncomprehendingly. "What about you? Come with me. We can go now."

He shook his head.

"You can't fight them! You've got nothing to fight them with!"

A grim smile curled his lips. "You'd be surprised."

Dalia stamped her foot angrily. "Damn it, Reuel! This is a hell of a time to decide to make war! Let's just go! We can arm ourselves, set a trap, and have the advantage!"

He studied her a long moment and she saw relief in his eyes that thoroughly confused her. "This *is* the trap, Dalia."

She gaped at him, but as he turned to go, she rushed after him. Grasping his wrist, she tugged on it until he stopped. When he did, she flung herself against him, holding tightly to him. "Be careful."

He peeled her loose and set her away from him, but caught her woebegone face between his palms and dropped a quick kiss on her lips. "I love you."

Chapter Thirteen

Sheer terror washed over Dalia as his words echoed hollowly through her mind.

He was going to die. He knew he was going to die or he would never have said that to her. Frantically, she looked around for the key. She'd been too stunned by everything that had happened within the past few moments to more than register the fact that he'd tossed it to her. She couldn't even remember catching it.

Had she caught it? Or had it landed on the floor, or the cot? Whirling, she headed back into the room. Just as she reached the doorway, however, two neutron bombs exploded overhead in quick succession. The concussion knocked her off her feet. Around her, the hut shuddered and began caving in. She covered her head, huddling in the door jam, hoping it was stronger than the rest of the hut had been. When the debris settled, she looked around her and found the quickest route out of the wreckage.

The morning sun was just cresting the horizon, throwing blood-red light over the compound. Above her, she saw it gleaming off of the domed force field that encompassed the entire compound.

She hadn't noticed it before because it hadn't been there.

Reuel had said this was the trap. She should have known! That was why everything had looked so thrown together and impermanent! That was why Reuel had said they would 'wait'. He hadn't been talking about the baby, not then, anyway. They were waiting for the company's militia. They'd known they would be followed.

Which meant that Reuel had known she was carrying another locator.

He'd been testing her, trying to find out if she was aware of it, and the fact that she'd been transmitting information to the company from the moment he'd picked her up.

Fury washed through her. She felt like choking him.

Damn the man anyway! He'd used her ... again!

Angrily, she glanced around for sight of him. The huts they'd built were piles of debris now. What caught her attention, however, were the cannons emerging from belowground ... and the three squads of cyborgs kneeling in battle formation behind them.

As she watched, a company craft appeared on the horizon, heading straight for them. Her heart leapt into her throat. They were going to have to drop the shield to fire on it and whoever was manning that ship knew it.

As small as the neutron bombs were that were used for localized battle, one would turn this entire compound into a pile of smoldering dust.

They were all mad!

They were all going to die.

She braced herself, knowing she didn't have enough time to run. As the craft shot over the palisade wall, the cyborg manning the largest of the cannons opened fire. White blue snakes of light shot upward like long, gnarled fingers, straight through the field, grabbing the craft. The craft dropped like a rock, bounced when it struck the field and began sliding along the curvature. The force field flickered and the craft dropped through, slamming into the ground with the sound of grinding metal.

Dalia was too stunned to move. As she watched, a squad of cyborgs leapt to their feet and charged the downed craft. Even as they reached it, a squad of rogue hunters stumbled out, stunned, bleeding, but struggling to form up.

They didn't get the chance. Before they could draw more than a ragged breath, the cyborgs fell upon them, beating any who refused to lay down their weapon into submission.

The discharge of the strange cannon brought Dalia's attention back to the cannons once more and she saw two more company craft shoot over the palisade and into the line of fire. "What is that thing?" she muttered. She'd thought it must be a neutron cannon, or perhaps a laser. Whatever it was, it had drained the propulsion from the craft as suddenly as if they'd flipped the off switch on the engine.

The two remaining cannons fired almost simultaneously. The first hit its target head on and that craft dropped, smashing into the force field. The second cannon missed its target entirely. That craft veered away, but she could see it was losing altitude fast. Even as the craft that had been struck dead on dropped through the force field and slammed into the ground, the third craft hit the trees beyond the palisade and exploded, sending shrapnel in every direction.

The effect was devastating. Debris shot through the opening before the force field could be reactivated, cutting down cyborg and rogue hunter alike. The distraction also cost them in domination of the field of battle. The squad of rogue hunters who piled out of the second ship was prepared for battle before the second squad of cyborgs could reach them. The hunters who'd been subdued, began struggling to free themselves to join the second squad.

As Dalia watched, Reuel leapt from the firing pad of the largest cannon and charged toward the fray, the final squad of cyborgs on his heels.

Dalia never consciously made the decision to join them. Her gaze followed Reuel and her heart and body followed. She was in the thick of the fight before she even realized that she had charged forward to help.

She was also completely unarmed.

It dawned upon her about the same moment that Reuel turned and caught a glimpse of her. Immediately distracted, he surged toward her. Dalia stared at him disbelievingly, but in the next moment, movement just to one side of him caught her attention and her gaze moved from Reuel to the man beside him. The hunter caught Reuel on the side of his jaw with the butt of his gun. Reuel's head jerked sideways at the impact and his body followed, flying toward the ground.

"No!" Dalia screamed, surging forward even as the hunter flipped his gun, switching ends and drawing a bead on Reuel, who was still struggling to rise. Launching herself at the man, she landed in the middle of his back. He staggered, but he was easily as big as Reuel and barely registered her attack. Locking her legs around his waist before he could toss her off, Dalia flipped the chain of the manacle around his neck, looped it once and pulled it taut. He gagged, bent forward belatedly to throw her over his head, and she tightened her legs around him.

He clawed at the chain, swung backwards, trying to knock her off. Despite her efforts to dodge him, he caught her along the jaw with the edge of his fist. Blackness swarmed at the edges of her vision, but she held on, pulling tautly at the chain until, finally, he dropped to his knees. When he did, she released her grip on his waist and kneed him in the back.

Someone caught her arm as the hunter fell face first onto the ground. She tried to shrug the hand off, gritting her teeth as she concentrated on choking the life out of the man. He caught her hair, jerking her head back. "Stop it, Dalia!"

She stared at Reuel blankly, but she didn't slacken her grip.

He caught her wrists. "We want captives, not dead men!"

The fight went out of her and she dropped her arms weakly. "He would've killed you."

Shaking his head, Reuel pulled her off of the unconscious man and hauled her away from the battle. He'd dragged her all the way back to the pile of rubble that had been her prison cell for the past three days before the shock wore off of Dalia enough for her to realize that he was furious as she had never seen him in all the weeks she'd known him. He surveyed the debris for several moments before he turned to look at her. She almost took a step back at the look in his eyes. "You gave me your word," he ground out.

Dalia blinked at him uncomprehendingly. "What?"

"I asked you to give me your word that you would protect my child, that you would leave if things went badly."

"Your child?" Dalia echoed, feeling dread seep into her.

His lips twisted. "Mine. If you had cared anything about it at all, you would not have joined the battle, without even a means of protecting yourself."

"I saved your life!" Dalia exclaimed, too stunned that he was attacking her even to feel any indignation.

Something flickered in his eyes, but his anger didn't abate. "*You* risked my life! You distracted me in the heat of battle. If you had done as I asked, if you'd done as you had given me your word you would, you wouldn't have been there to start with.

"Have you no conception of how fragile the life is that you carry? Or does it simply not matter to you?"

Dalia stared at him, feeling horror wash over her in a cold tide as a dozen images flickered through her mind of past battles she'd engaged in, the blows she'd taken, the wounds. Almost any one of those could have meant the death of her baby.

As badly as she wanted to dispute his hurtful remarks, she couldn't. He was right. She hadn't thought about the baby. She had acted, just as she had always acted, as if she was no more than a mindless machine behaving as programmed, without any ability to make her own judgments, her own decisions.

And not once had she thought about the tiny life inside of her. What kind of mother would she be if she thoughtlessly endangered the life of her child?

She should have done what he'd said she must do, or at least stayed as far away from the fighting, and danger, as she possibly could. She hadn't given him her word. She'd been too worried about him even then to consider what he was saying, but it hardly mattered. The baby was completely and utterly dependent upon her now merely to sustain life. If she'd sustained a mortal blow, it, too, would have died.

He was right about the other, as well, she realized. She *had* distracted him. He'd asked her to promise she would protect the child and then she'd joined the battle, distracted him, and almost gotten him killed.

Guilt fell over her shoulders, crushing the air from her lungs. She found she couldn't sustain the look in his eyes any longer and dropped her gaze to her hands. He grasped her chin, forcing her to look at him. "Is that your answer? Nothing?"

What was she supposed to say? It did matter, but how could she argue that it did after what she'd done? Or should she just agree that her actions were sufficient in themselves to prove that, whatever else she felt about it, she was too used to thinking only of herself, and for herself, to consider the possible consequences? "I can't see that there's anything to say," she managed finally.

If anything, it seemed her response only made him angrier. Grasping her arm, he walked her across the compound to the group of cyborgs that was rounding up the hunters. "Put her with the rest of them. When you've secured them in the hold, look for survivors. The craft went down slow enough some of them might have bailed."

The cyborg he'd spoken to took her arm, glancing from her to Reuel with a puzzled frown. "You're going after the other craft?"

Reuel nodded grimly. "We can't afford to let them get back to the company. If we're not back by the time you've finished here, leave. We'll see you when we get back to Mordal."

Although Dalia nerved herself to look at him, hoping that his anger had abated, he didn't so much as glance at her before he left. She supposed she should've been relieved that he hadn't looked at her again considering the look in is eyes before. Instead, it only made the guilt weigh more heavily upon her.

After a few moments, the cyborg led her toward an enormous cargo ship that seemed to have appeared out of nowhere. Surprise briefly filtered through her misery, but it dimmed almost as quickly. Obviously the whole compound had been nothing more than a stage above the real compound. She'd been carefully placed far enough from where they were making their preparations to keep her from seeing what they were doing, to keep her from knowing that the handful of cyborgs she'd seen were only a fraction of the number actually here.

It seemed indisputable that Reuel had not only known she had another locator, but he'd believed she was a part of the company's plan to discover the rebel compound. Otherwise there would have been no reason to make sure she didn't know what the plan was.

She frowned at that, wondering when the company had decided she would be more useful in leading them to the rebels than dead. She didn't believe that the attempt on her life had been faked, but it was possible it had. The company was devious if nothing else and Reuel said they had discovered his plant weeks before they discovered that she'd conceived.

It made sense now that she considered all the pieces. Whether they managed to get any information out of the cyborg they'd caught or not, they had to know something was up and that it involved her. Once they had discovered that she had been successfully impregnated, they'd have to know that that made her invaluable to the cyborgs. All they had to do was make her run for her life, make sure it was on all the open channels that they were hunting her down to kill her and wait for the cyborgs to pick her up and take her back to the colony.

Somewhere in the rounds, they'd taken the extra precaution, she supposed, of implanting another locator, one she had no knowledge of. Or, maybe, considering the way the company operated, it had been there all along?

They had underestimated Reuel. He'd been two steps ahead of them all the way, waltzing his pieces across the chessboard as if he were clairvoyant and knew everything they would do before they did it.

The company's determination to wipe the cyborgs out had given the cyborgs the opportunity to 'free' the hunters from the company's control and nix any further attacks, for the foreseeable future anyway.

Of course, she supposed complete victory hinged on Reuel managing to catch the last ship before they managed to get away.

The cyborg led her up the gangplank and down a long corridor. Once inside, she saw it was a lab. She was striped and ordered to lie down on a table. She did as she was told, without questioning it. Ignoring the tech, who moved around her extracting blood and checking the fetus' vital signs, she studied the ceiling lights and finally turned to look around the room. She saw then that there was a row of similar tables all the way to the far wall, separated only by a narrow strip of sheeting hung from hooks on the ceiling. A hunter was strapped to each, some being treated for wounds, others merely being examined.

Finally, she was rolled onto her stomach and the tech extracted the 'hidden' locator that had been attached to her spine.

When they'd finished, a flimsy gown was handed to her that tied around the neck and overlapped in the back to tie around her waist. Then she was escorted from the lab, along the corridor and down a flight of stairs. The compartment she found herself in was lined with cots. Hers was in one corner. She made her way to it and sat down, staring at nothing in particular, feeling curiously numb.

They hadn't even told her if the baby was all right. She was tempted to access her inboard computer to assess it, but it occurred to her that it really didn't have enough data to tell her anything more than whether or not the baby was still alive and growing.

She decided she didn't want to know.

"Dalia?"

Dalia turned to look at the woman who'd called her name. It took several moments for recognition to set in. The name continued to elude her however. "How are you?"

The woman shrugged. "Just bruised and banged up a bit. I'll live."

For some reason, that struck Dalia as funny. She snorted.

"You know something I don't?"

Dalia shrugged. "I don't remember your name."

The woman looked surprised for a moment, then frowned. "We trained together. Camile?"

Dalia nodded. "I remember. It's just ... actually I never really paid much attention to anyone's name. I figured it wasn't a good idea to get to know anyone, considering...."

Camile shrugged. "I guess I can see your point." She frowned. "I couldn't help but notice you were fighting with them, not against them. What'd they do, brainwash you?"

"They told me the truth."

Camile's brows rose. "What truth?"

"That I ... that we, are the same as they are." She glanced around at the hunters nearest them. "We're cyborgs."

Chapter Fourteen

"Speak for yourself, you traitorous bitch! You might be nothing more than a stinking machine, but I'm sure as hell not!"

Dalia stared at the woman across the aisle from her and Camile, recognizing her as one of those who'd trained with her. "Think about it, Zenia. Do you really think the company would risk precious *human* lives to clean up their mess? And what human would be able to single-handedly take on a cyborg?"

The woman made an abortive attempt to leap up from her cot, but Dalia saw she was chained to it. She wasn't surprised. Zenia was probably the most unstable, and most fierce of all the female hunters. Her problem had always been that she completely lost it when she went into a fight. It was for that reason that, despite her skills, and her determination, she'd been defeated by the cyborgs she'd been sent to eliminate more times than she'd succeeded. She'd been patched up and put back together by the company so many times that even if she'd been born human, she was more machine now than anything else.

"I've taken down my share," Zenia gritted out.

Dalia's lips curled. "Your logic circuits should have been replaced a long time ago. If you're too stupid to grasp that, then think about this--Zenia. It's a flower. Camile, Dalia. Do you think your parents just happened to name you after a flower and you just happened to end up in the hunter program? All of us? Every female in the hunter program bears the name of a flower. Doesn't that seem like just too much of a coincidence to be a coincidence?"

"I remember my childhood," Camile said quietly.

"You remember what they imbedded in our programming. None of it happened to you. It happened to someone else, or it was computer generated. I don't know that much, but I do know it's true. Do you think I like it any better than you do? Do you know something I don't? If you know something that proves beyond a shadow of doubt that the company didn't lie to us, tell me. Because I'd much rather believe that I'm human."

Camile frowned, but she had paled. Like Zenia, she looked vaguely ill. "They said you were gestating. That the cyborgs had found a way to simulate reproduction."

Dalia sighed. Drawing her knees up, she covered her face with her hands. "We're the next generation CO479, the new and improved model. They decided the CO479s had gone rogue because of faulty programming. So we were designed to be *more* human, to believe we were human. You shouldn't be at all surprised to know they fucked up-- again. They made me, us, so human that the biological engineering took prominence. All of the human organs and glands they engineered for us began functioning in a purely human way, or purely biological way. Reproduction is part of that cycle. When they failed to include the critical materials for reproduction, our bodies, probably because of the rapid cell regeneration we were given, were able to improvise and evolve ... or at least mine did. I'm betting we will all find that we've evolved reproduction capabilities.

"It's why the cyborgs were determined to capture all of you alive. We're the same, except we have a future and they don't. Maybe they figure they can discover what's missing from them so they can change it.

"I honestly don't know what the ultimate plan is, or even if there is one. All I do know is that they feel like, as cyborgs, we belong together, and, to their way of thinking, they have freed us from human bondage."

Zenia made a sneering sound and rattled the chain attached to her wrist. "If they'd asked me, I'd have told them I preferred human bondage. At least they didn't keep me in chains," she growled.

Dalia lifted her head and stared at Zenia a long moment. "You're so very reasonable, Zenia. I'm sure they'll realize very quickly that you, of all of us, don't need time to adjust--or even reprogramming."

Camile snickered, but tried to disguise it as a cough.

Zenia, naturally enough, took exception to the remark and began screaming profanity. Shrugging disinterestedly, Dalia laid down and turned her back on the woman. The snub only infuriated her more and she began beating the chain, trying to break it. After a few moments, three cyborgs marched into the room. One grasped her by either arm. The third injected her with something, and blessed peace settled over the hold.

There was nothing to mark the passage of time beyond the meals that were brought in and since Dalia didn't know the schedule, even that didn't help much. Two meals were delivered and then five more cyborgs were brought into the holding cell on stretchers.

Dalia thought they might be survivors of the craft that had crashed, but none of them were in any condition to communicate.

The lights were dimmed for a while and she slept. She was awakened hours later by the delivery of another meal. Several hours later, a large group of hunters was led in. Dalia sat up, examining them as they passed.

"That's Lincoln. I saw Clinton and Kennedy, too. They were on the Valiant4."

Dalia glanced over at Camile. "The craft that managed to get away?"

Camile grimaced. "Obviously not."

Dalia settled back against the bunk, staring at the ceiling while she fought to still the frantic pounding of her heart. Reuel had come back. She hadn't realized how worried she'd been that he wouldn't until that moment, until she felt the terrible need to give vent to tears. She was still struggling with it when a stray thought abruptly popped into her mind. Amusement replaced the desire to cry and a chuckle escaped her.

"What?"

"The presidents. They named the males after presidents."

Camile stared at her blankly for several moments and finally chuckled. She sobered almost at once. "It's true, isn't it? What you said?"

Dalia sighed. "If I hadn't believed it, I wouldn't have said it. Sometimes, I'm still not sure I do, but maybe it's because I don't want to, not because there's any room for doubt."

They'd just finished what Dalia thought was their evening meal when the bulkheads began to shudder and the sound of revving engines drowned the conversations within the hold. Almost as one, they looked around and then up at the ceiling, watching the lights above them flicker as power was diverted into the launch engines. The shuddering increased, became a hard rattle as the ship sluggishly lifted from the ground.

An invisible weight settled over them, pressing harder and harder until, abruptly, it ceased as they broke the planet's gravity. For a handful of seconds disorientation set in and then artificial gravity kicked in and the sickening sense of imbalance disappeared.

Thereafter, the days seemed to meld one into another. Once they'd taken off, guards came through the room and released those who'd been restrained, including, unfortunately, Zenia. They were allowed to roam the hold, but not beyond it, except for twice a day when they were herded through the particle showers.

After perhaps a week, they began allowing the hunters to leave the hold in small groups to spend part of the day in the recreation room, but it was strictly for the hunters. Except for the guards in the viewing rooms above them, they saw none of the cyborgs. Dalia was disappointed, but not really surprised. She thought it was probably just as well. She didn't particularly relish the thought of another encounter with Reuel. She would've liked, however, to know for certain that he'd survived.

She tried not to think about the baby as the weeks passed. Reuel had indicated that she'd forfeited her right to have anything to do with it after its birth. It was almost a relief. Until he'd pointed out how unfit she was to mother a child, she'd been afraid to acknowledge her self-doubts, but the truth was, she hadn't been designed for such a thing and she was not only afraid it wasn't something she could learn, she was fearful of the results of any efforts on her part. She didn't know much about infants, but she did know that they were fragile and easily damaged.

What if she were to drop it? What if she fed it too much or fed it the wrong thing? What if it became ill? They couldn't talk, not at first, anyway. What if it needed something and she couldn't figure out what that was?

Just thinking about it scared her worse than anything had ever frightened her in her life. She was afraid of the birthing part, too, but not nearly as much. She knew how to deal with pain. She hadn't engaged in fifty battles over the past three years and she hadn't come off of all of them completely unscathed.

Apart from the fear, thinking about the baby made her feel indescribably sad. It seemed grossly unfair that nature had seen fit to give her the ability to reproduce and not given her any of the instincts or knowledge for mothering it. She had only to reference other living organisms in nature, however, to know that that wasn't altogether uncommon even in other creatures. Reptiles didn't nurture their young. There were even some species of mammals and birds that had little or no nurturing instincts, and, as often as not, failed to rear their offspring to maturity.

Shuddering at the thought, she realized that the best tact was to simply ignore it as much as she could.

That became more and more difficult as the weeks passed, however. The gestation didn't follow the rules of human gestation. The fetus was developing at an accelerated rate. Her in board computer calculated maturity in little more than twenty weeks at its current rate and possibly less.

Not only was her belly ballooning almost before her eyes, but the odd little flutters she'd first felt quickly became uncomfortable punches in some very sensitive internal areas. By the time they'd been in the hold by her best guess, a month, the activity beneath her shift was sufficient to draw all eyes as she passed, even if they were polite enough to ignore the growing bulge.

Boredom, sadness and worry weren't her only companions, unfortunately. Zenia had focused all of her fear of her situation, and all of her grief over her loss of 'humanity' into a fixated hatred of Dalia. After the incident when the guards had sedated her, she'd made it a point to keep her distance, but she stared at Dalia with hatred in her eyes, leaving her in no doubt that, sooner or later, Zenia would strike.

At any other time, she would almost have relished a physical confrontation, if only to relieve her boredom, but she'd learned her lesson. Danger for her meant danger for the fetus and she couldn't risk it. Beyond that, she shuddered to think what Reuel would do to her if she were to find herself in the middle of another battle, whether it was of her making or not. At any rate, it was impossible to ignore the fact that the bigger the infant grew, the slower, clumsier and more vulnerable she became. If she were not burdened by the infant, she knew she could best Zenia in any contest of skills. In her current condition, she couldn't.

Camile was friendly enough, but Dalia doubted it would occur to her to help if Zenia crossed the line and attacked. The same was true of most of the others. They were trained warriors. They might watch two warriors battle it out with interest, but it certainly wouldn't occur to them to feel any need to intervene.

There was also the insurmountable fact that, on varying levels, she wasn't particularly popular, even among the hunters. Some of the resentment predated her involvement in the affairs of the cyborgs, to her hunting days, and was directly proportional to her success as a hunter-- professional jealousy. Zenia wasn't by any means the only one who'd viewed her helping the cyborgs as treachery, either, and then there were those who resented her merely for being the bearer of bad tidings.

All in all, it was only the fact that they were constantly watched, and knew it, that had kept any number of them from working out their fears and frustrations on her.

Pierce was the exception. They'd been in the hold almost three weeks before she even realized that he was among those captured. He hadn't approached her, but when she'd finally emerged from her abstraction enough to notice, she realized that he had been watching her for some time.

They'd come as close to being friends in their early days of training as anyone ever did, and even for a while after they'd emerged from training and begun assignments. The company didn't encourage friendships. And their training and the demands of the job made it nearly impossible anyway. She'd scarcely seen him in the past two years and usually only then in passing.

She knew, however, that Pierce felt more than friendship toward her. If anyone would be willing to help her, he would.

The thoughts had barely formed in her mind before doubts crept in. She might never have considered him in a sexual light, but she liked Pierce, very much, and it wasn't right to use him, even knowing it might be a matter of survival. There was also the little matter of Reuel. It seemed unlikely he would care. It seemed unlikely, now, that anything would come of what had happened between them before, but she still felt bound to him, felt like it would be betraying him to even consider becoming friendly with another man.

She wrestled with it for almost two weeks, but in the end she knew she had no choice. The trip seemed interminable. The ship had been designed for long hauls of huge cargoes, not speed, and there was no telling how long they would be imprisoned together in the hold.

Finally, nerving herself, she approached Pierce in the rec room. Almost from the moment she started in his direction, his gaze fell to her bulging abdomen and remained fixed there until she felt so awkward and hideous it took all she could do to refrain from whirling and bolting in the other direction. "Hi," she said, smiling with an effort.

Pierce turned red and stumbled from his seat, knocking his chair over in the process. "Dalia! It is you," he said, and then turned even redder. "What I meant was, I hardly recogniz.... No. What I meant was ... shit!"

Agonizingly aware that a half a dozen people were watching them, Dalia smiled with an effort. "I hope that means you're glad to see me."

He laughed, dragged a hand through his shaggy blond hair and finally swarmed toward her and grabbed her in an awkward embrace, rocking her slightly. "I am glad to see you, Dally. God I've missed you!"

"Step away from the female!"

Pierce released her as if he'd just discovered he was holding a hot piece of metal and jumped back. He glared up at the observation window.

Dalia placed a hand on his arm warningly. "Never mind."

He looked at her, still frowning, but finally a grin dawned. He was taller than she remembered, blonder. She realized she'd forgotten how handsome he was, or, more accurately, she supposed she'd never really noticed. She *had* noticed that one out of every two females that glanced his way did a double take, or simply stopped dead in her tracks and gaped at him as he walked by, but he'd never had that effect on her, never made her heart flutter with excitement. It was unfortunate, because he was as kind as he was handsome and he always made her laugh.

He'd always reminded her of a frisky puppy--a very large frisky puppy--always anxious to please, delighted with the smallest scrap of attention.

She immediately felt ten times worse than she had when she'd considered renewing their friendship merely for safety's sake. As he grabbed her arm and led her to an empty couch, however, she realized that it wasn't only for that reason. Until Reuel, she'd never been close to any other person, but, in the time they'd spent together, she'd grown accustomed to having someone to talk to, to touch and she desperately missed contact with another breathing being.

Pierce, she noticed, was beaming at her, watching her expectantly. His gaze kept flicking toward her belly, however. "So--it's true what they said about you then? Man! I can't believe my little Dally's going to be a mom!"

Dalia blushed uncomfortably. "I suppose by 'they' you mean the company?"

He shrugged. "Bunch of assholes. I won't miss it. I can tell you that. I never did have the stomach for ... well, hell, I never was any good at it anyway."

"That's not true! If you hadn't been, you would've been cut from the program."

Again, he shrugged dismissively. "Oh, I never had any problem learning the skills. I can't say I even mind a rousing good fight from time to time, but I puked my guts out every time I had to kill."

Dalia looked at him in surprise. "You too?"

He laughed, but the sound had no humor in it. "I kept trying to convince myself they were just machines and it wasn't any different from busting up a ... freezing unit or something like that, but it was ... the blood, the look in their eyes.

Throwing a glance in the direction of the viewing windows again, he leaned toward her. "Can I feel it?"

Dalia looked at him blankly. "Feel what?"

"The little tyke."

"The what?"

He gave her an exasperated look. "The baby, Dally."

Dalia studied at him self-consciously, but finally nodded. Pierce placed his hand on her rounded stomach and frowned in concentration. After a moment, he grinned. "It's an active little thing. My mom told me.... Uh." He broke off, looking at her uncomfortably. "Forgot."

Dalia hated seeing the glow of happiness in his eyes dim. "Never mind, Pierce. What did she tell you?"

He looked at her a little hopefully. "Boys are more active. She was ... she was really old fashioned. She had all of us herself. She said it wasn't natural to breed babies in tanks, like they were goldfish or something."

He looked so unhappy; she cast around in her mind for something to distract him. Unfortunately, nothing came to mind. "You like babies?"

He smiled. "Sure. They're cute as hell. I had...." He broke off again and leaned back against the couch, staring up at the ceiling. "This really confuses the hell out of me, Dally. I don't know now what happened and what didn't. I was beginning to think that me and you being friends was only more of the memory implant. You didn't seem to recognize me. I can't tell you what pure hell it was to think I'd lost ...my best little buddy."

Guilt swamped her. He didn't have to tell her what he was thinking and feeling. His face was as open and honest as Reuel's was dark and mysterious. "I'm so sorry! I didn't mean to ignore you, it's just ... I've been so unhappy since we were put in here that I was too self-absorbed even to realize you were here."

He rolled his head along the back of the couch and studied her for several moments. Finally, he sat forward, grasping her hand. "Hey! You shouldn't be unhappy. You're going to be a mom!"

As much as she appreciated his efforts to cheer her, pointing out the one thing that was making her most unhappy didn't help. Regardless, it was sweet of him and, impulsively, Dalia leaned toward him and kissed him on the cheek.

"Release the female!"

Dalia whirled at the voice that barked at them over the speakers, looking up toward the viewing window. Reuel was standing at the window, looking directly at her, his expression almost a mirror of the last she'd seen--one of pure fury.

Chapter Fifteen

Fear and guilt hit Dalia a good five seconds before outrage. She jerked away from Pierce before the thoughts even connected in her mind. Pierce reacted almost identically, which only added to Dalia's irritation when indignation finally hit her. Dalia jumped to her feet and turned to glare up at Reuel, her hands on her hips. "What? Is fucking not allowed among the prisoners?"

Dalia knew the moment the words were out of her mouth that she'd been spoiling for a fight and hoping to provoke one. She also knew, just from the look on Reuel's face, that it would've been wiser to chose another point of contention.

Most of the hunters in the room merely gaped at her, but several of them snickered.

Reuel looked like he might explode.

Pierce, she saw when she glanced at him, was staring at her with his mouth at half cock. "Majia's balls, Dalia! You want to get us thrown into solitary confinement or something?"

"Wait a minute," the hunter, Kennedy, said, getting to his feet. "She's got a point. If we're not company men anymore, if we're free men, then we ought to be able to socialize with our fellow hunters if we want to, *any* way we want to."

"We haven't been told anything," Rose put in, standing up and addressing the cyborgs in the viewing room above them, as well. "Dalia said we were to be part of the cyborg community. Why are we still being held prisoner if that's the case?"

Dalia glanced at Rose and then around at the others in the room uneasily. She hadn't intended to start a riot, but it looked as if one was brewing. "Because we've given them no reason to believe they can trust us, and every reason to believe we still see them as our enemies."

The comment drew the attention of everyone near enough to hear. Rose looked at her curiously and finally spoke again. "Why are you here? With us, I mean? The company said you'd gone rogue. You fought with them, against us. It seems to me that that means they'll never trust us, or accept us. And, if that's the case, why take us at all?"

Dalia shook her head and lowered her voice. "It wasn't like you thought it was."

Rose glanced up at the viewing room and moved closer. "Then what was it? Why did you try to kill Jackson?"

"I wasn't fighting for them, or against you. I was trying to help someone I cared for. It was against orders and they've no tolerance for mistakes, and no forgiveness."

Rose glanced toward the guards again uneasily. "If that's true, they're no better than the company."

Dalia shrugged. "And no worse."

"She means, they won't accept us, no matter what," Kennedy said.

Dalia glanced around at the others a little helplessly. "Trust takes time. They're willing to try or they would've simply killed you all and been done with it. They could've done it, easily. You saw the weapon they've developed. All they would've had to do was drain the ships of power and let them hit the cliffs. If you're willing to try, then eventually, you'll find a place for yourself."

"What if we're not willing? What if we don't want to build a cyborg nation? Is this 'freeing' us going to still be an option? Or are we only 'free' men as long as we believe what they believe?"

Dalia glanced toward the man who'd spoken. "I don't honestly know. They never said, but I got the impression that they meant to release anyone who didn't fit in to go their own way."

"As far as the company is concerned, we're rogues now, not hunters. It looks to me like we can stay with the rogues or be hunted. That doesn't give us much freedom of choice."

Dalia drew in an annoyed breath. "That's the only freedom of choice anybody's ever had," she snapped. "And it's more that you had. I don't know about the rest of you, but I was inducted. I didn't decide to be a hunter. I made the best of it because I didn't particularly care for the consequences of failure, but it was never my *choice!*"

Feeling a hand along her waist, Dalia glanced back sharply, and saw with relief that Pierce had come to stand protectively behind her. "Give her a break! She doesn't know any more than we do."

She was relieved when the others drifted off, returning to their own interests. She didn't glance up at the booth again, but Pierce's hand on her waist began to feel like a firebrand. After a moment, she moved away from him. Taking a seat on the couch once more, she turned, putting her back against the arm at one end and placing her knee on the seat between them. Pierce glanced at her, shrugged, and moved to the opposite end.

She couldn't help but grin at him. He grinned back. "Somebody up there's feeling damned possessive, Dally," he murmured almost lazily, though something flickered in the depths of his deep blue eyes that told her he didn't feel nearly as unperturbed by it as he was determined to pretend.

She frowned, but instead of addressing the comment, said, "I never told you, I know, but I never particularly cared for being called Dally."

He grinned mischievously at her and chuckled. "I know."

She stared at him in surprise, then started laughing. "I'd forgotten you were such a tease."

His brows rose, something a bit warmer than friendship gleaming in them. "Now I'm hurt. When I think of all the hours I wasted thinking up things to do to aggravate the hell out of you!"

"Pierce!" she clamped a hand over her mouth, realizing she'd practically shrieked his name. "That was you that put peroxide in my toothpaste! You ass! I thought I'd been poisoned when I started foaming at the mouth."

He gave her a sheepish grin. "OK, so I fucked up. I put too much in it. That's why I never told you it was me."

She glared at him several moments and then snickered. "I knew it was you. That's why I put alum in yours."

He burst out laughing. "I hope you know I beat the pure hell out of poor Grant for that."

Dalia grimaced. "I know. That's why I never told you it was me."

He shrugged, his eyes still gleaming with amusement. "He deserved it anyway, the asshole. I never did like that son-of-a-bitch."

She cast her mind back to their days together in training, the incident under discussion in particular, and chuckled and the memory. "You looked so cute with your mouth all puckered up from the alum."

"Right! That's why I got slapped by three different females before I could get out of the shower room. They thought I was making lewd faces at them."

"Oh!" Dalia commented, covering her mouth with her hands and trying to look suitably repentant. She failed. Despite her best efforts, she burst out laughing and kept laughing until tears were streaming down her face. "Oh, I'm so sorry, Pierce," she said when she could catch her breath.

"No you're not," he said without rancor. "You'd have laughed yourself silly about it then, if you'd known it, you heartless baggage."

Dalia mopped the tears from her cheeks, stifling the urge to laugh with an effort. "I am."

His eyes gleamed. A slow smile curled his lips. "Paybacks are hell, you know."

"You wouldn't!" Dalia said, managing to give him a wide-eyed look of remorse.

"You needn't bat those beautiful brown eyes at me. You know I've always been a sucker for you, baby, but nothing will save you now. Those females still glare at me every time they see me."

"Well!" she said indignantly. "You got me first, remember?"

He laughed. "Yes, but you got me better."

She bit her lip to keep from smiling back. "Are they here?"

He rolled his eyes. "Yeah, they're here."

"You're serious? You're not making it up?"

"Which part?"

"The slap."

His eyes gleamed and she knew he'd been teasing her. "Maybe I exaggerated a little bit."

"How little?" Dalia asked suspiciously.

He sighed. "All right. I only got slapped once, but I did get glared at. The main thing is, it made you laugh. I always loved the way you laughed, Dally."

Dalia's heart skidded uncomfortably at the look in his eyes. Despite the teasing way he'd said it, she realized suddenly that he meant it. He'd always meant it, all the times he'd looked at her in just that way and said 'I love your eyes'; 'I love your hair'; 'You're beautiful'--he'd been saying 'I love you'.

It was disconcerting the transformation that seemed to occurred right before her eyes. He looked the same--blond, gorgeous, playful and addicted to teasing and annoying pranks, but quite suddenly she ceased to feel almost as if he were her brother and saw him as a very desirable man.

Why was it that everyone else had seen what she'd been blind to? The programming? Or had she just been too close? Had distance and time and the situation changed the way she felt? Or was it because Reuel had opened the door to passion and then deprived her of it? And, if that was so, was it mere animal attraction? Or more?

She looked away from him uncomfortably. "Is she here?"

"The psycho woman? Yeah, she's here. Still looks at me like she wants to boil me in oil or something."

Dalia was instantly distracted from her uncomfortable new awareness of Pierce. "Zenia?"

"How'd you guess?"

She sighed shakily. "She looks at me the same way."

Pierce sat up, all traces of humor gone. "What'd you do to piss her off?"

Dalia shrugged. "Breathe, I think."

Pierce looked her over searchingly. "You're not worried about her, are you? Because I know you can kick her ass any day of the week."

"I could. I can't now."

His gaze dropped to her belly and remained there for several moments. Finally, he reached across the couch and caught her hand, giving it a squeeze before he released it and sat back. "Don't worry about it, Dally. I'm your man."

Relief seemed to roll off of her like a boulder. "Thanks!"

He grinned. "If she so much as looks at you in a way I don't like--I'll grab you up and run like hell."

Dalia chuckled. "Good. I don't think I could outrun her by myself right now."

He waggled his eyebrows at her. "And, by the way, since you brought it up, if you think you might be interested in fucking, I'm your man there, too."

Dalia chuckled dutifully, but despite the fact that he'd said it jokingly, she realized joking had always been a smoke screen for Pierce to hide his behind. He was making it clear that he wanted to be considered if she intended to look for a lover.

When they returned to the holding cell, Pierce walked to the opposite end, collected his belongings and returned, depositing them on the floor beside her cot. She looked at him in surprise. "Not enough cots. I guess there was more of us than they were expecting, but I figure the floor's as comfortable at this end as the other."

For the first time since they'd been confined, Dalia actually managed to sleep deeply. The following morning when she woke, she discovered that Zenia's cot was empty.

She sat up and glanced around in surprise.

"The guards took her last night," Camile volunteered.

Dalia felt her jaw go slack. "They just took her?"

Camile shrugged. "They were in and out so fast, I wouldn't have seen it except that I've been sleeping with one eye on her. What do you think it means?"

"It means we don't have to worry about the psycho bitch anymore," Pierce said, yawning hugely and scratching his head as he sat up. "And everything we say is heard."

Dalia looked at him sharply. "You think so?" she asked quickly, mentally reviewing their conversation the day before.

Pierce shrugged. "Like you said, they've got no reason to trust us, and every reason not to. I know if I had nearly a hundred prisoners I was transporting, I'd want to keep up with what was going on."

"What do you think they'll do with her?" Camile asked nervously.

Pierce sent her a look. "You're not going to pretend you care?"

She glared at him. "She's not a ... rabid animal that can just be put down."

"She doesn't miss it by much," Pierce said dryly. "Look, I know what you're saying, but the company would've fixed the problem if it was fixable. You've been around her long enough to know she's dangerously unstable."

"Yes, but--she's a human--she's a being. If they do something to her, what's to stop them from doing the same to the rest of us?"

"We're not psychotic?"

Camile threw her pillow at his head.

"If it was me, I'd ship her back to the company. They deserve her. She's their problem."

Dalia said nothing, but she felt uneasy about it, wondering if it was something she'd said. She didn't like to think she might be responsible if they did decide to terminate Zenia.

She watched the guards as they brought in the morning meal, but none of them seemed to pay her any more attention than any of the others. After they'd gone through the particle baths, however, the guards rounded up nearly half the men, including Pierce, and marched them out.

The place was strangely quiet without them even though no one had been inclined to talk much since they'd been imprisoned. When the noon meal came and went without any sign of them, Dalia wasn't alone in her increasing anxiety. Finally, late in the day, the men returned. All of them were tired and filthy, but Dalia was so glad to see that Pierce was among them she it took an effort to keep from bursting into tears and throwing her arms around him. The only reason she restrained herself was her certainty that Pierce was right. They were being monitored.

"You're all right?" she asked anxiously when he dropped down beside her bunk.

He nodded, then threw her a tired grin. "They had us cleaning out a new section all day. Looks like they mean to take care of the overcrowding problem."

Camile and Dalia exchanged a look. "You think so?"

"I hope they didn't have us lugging all that stuff around for nothing."

He seemed so certain, that Dalia felt her anxiety diminish.

None of them were greatly surprised, therefore, when they'd finished the evening meal and been herded through the particle baths once more to discover that some of them would be moving to new quarters. They were surprised when they learned it would only be the females.

Pierce, Dalia realized feeling a surge of anger, had been right. Everything they'd said the day before had been heard, and everything they'd done observed. Reuel didn't want her, but he wasn't about to let her be with anyone else.

Pierce was angry, as well, but not so much because he would be deprived of Dalia's company as he was because the move prevented him from watching over her. He could complain, of course, but he doubted it would do any good. Instead, after studying Camile speculatively for some moments, he pulled her aside. "I need to ask a favor of you."

Camile looked him over suspiciously. "What?"

"Look out for my little Dally for me. Ordinarily, I wouldn't worry about her, but she can't defend herself right now. I'm a dead man if anything happens to her because I'm going to have to kill somebody, but I'd much rather prevent it."

Camile nodded, but then shrugged. "I would have anyway," she said, smiling faintly.

Chapter Sixteen

After nearly three months, Dalia woke to the sensations that told her the cargo ship had arrived at last at its destination. At first, she thought the scarcely noticeable vibration was no more than the shudder of an engine, or the hull of the ship being pelted by micro meteors. The vibration increased steadily, however, quickly becoming a hard rattling that was impossible to interpret as anything but a descent into a gravitational field.

Sitting up, she looked around at the vibrating walls of the bulkheads and then at the faces of the other women who shared the compartment with her. Their fears and uncertainty reflected her own.

They'd arrived. Would they be freed? Or would they find that they were only exchanging one prison for another?

"Do you think they'll let us out?" Camile asked, voicing her own question.

"Some, at least--I think," Dalia responded cautiously.

As they had when she'd first been captured, the cyborgs had begun to allow them the run of the ship in small numbers and for short periods after they'd been kept isolated for more than a month.

It was as effective a strategy on most of the hunters as it had been on her. The natural fear of the unknown, coupled with incarceration, had made them cautious of their freedom, and careful not to abuse it. They were openly watched, of course, and certain areas were still off limits, but being allowed even so much after so long was enough to make them grateful. The cyborgs were neither welcoming nor hostile, but that, too, seemed almost calculating, as if they knew the hunters would be suspicious of any overtures of friendship.

Little by little, they had begun to relax their guard, to feel less like prisoners and more like mutual travelers. She'd noticed that some had even begun to form tentative friendships among the cyborgs. There was no reason that she could see that the cyborgs would consider it necessary to continue to imprison them.

Even if they'd wanted to leave, none of them had any idea of where they'd been taken. They had no way to leave short of stealing the ship they'd just spent the past three months on, and she rather thought most of the hunters would prefer almost anything to spending three more months on it.

The truth was that Dalia was *almost* certain that most of the hunters would find themselves absorbed into the cyborg community immediately. There were others, however, who wouldn't, some who might never be accepted and that was the part that worried her. What would happen to those who wanted nothing to do with the cyborgs? Would they simply 'disappear'? Or would the cyborgs, as Reuel had hinted, simply take them elsewhere and leave them?

She couldn't help but wonder if she fell into the latter category--not because the cyborgs in general didn't accept her, because they seemed far more welcoming toward her than any of the other hunters, but because Reuel, in particular, didn't accept her.

Reuel had been most conspicuous by his absence. She didn't think it was purely coincidence that he was rarely to be seen when she was allowed the freedom of the ship. She thought he was aware of everything that happened on the ship, including the schedules and that he made certain he was occupied elsewhere when she was allowed out.

She wasn't certain why. It hardly seemed necessary. He'd made his position clear enough the last time he'd spoken to her. It might still hurt. She might still care, but she certainly had no intention of making either of them uncomfortable by forcing any sort of confrontation.

Of course, she supposed, after the incident in the rec room, he might have reason to think a chance meeting could get ugly.

She might have been tempted except that that incident had cost her Pierce's company and she didn't particularly relish the thought of giving Reuel any reason for further retaliation. She missed Pierce almost as desperately as she missed Reuel. Having someone for companionship would have made the trip less unbearable. It would have left her less time to dwell on unpleasant memories, to worry about things beyond her control. She'd caught no more than a glimpse of Pierce from time to time after they were separated, and she knew that that was Reuel's doing, most likely because she'd very nearly created a serious disturbance by her outburst.

As the vibration of descent became a hard rattle and then a gentle bumping and finally a horrendous bucking that threatened whiplash, Dalia clung to her cot and mentally clocked their descent through the atmosphere. As many times as she had made descents, each and every one terrified her as much as the one before. The bucking was a very graphic expression of having reached the absolute peak of danger. From the time the ship began until at last the bucking slowed to the occasional jolt or sudden, weightless drop, she could never manage to do anything but listen intently to every rattling bolt, waiting to see if something would break off and send them spiraling planetward at a speed that insured that their grave marker would be a crater.

Sighing in relief when they at last passed through the critical zone, Dalia consciously peeled her fingers loose from the bars of the cot and sat up once more. She was almost immediately sorry she had, for the artificial gravity was disengaged at that moment and a wave of nausea rushed over her. She lay back again, closing her eyes and waiting for the planet's gravity to right her internal gyro.

She could feel the ship dropping steadily and wondered if they'd entered the atmosphere close to their destination or if they might expect hours more of cruising before they landed at last. Concentrating on that instead of the sickness, she almost felt as if she could count the miles they dropped, see the land rushing up toward them.

The gravity was noticeably different.

It was a smaller world than Earth then, almost certainly, but not much. Or, perhaps, the planet spun more slowly? Or the sun that warmed it was more distant?

When the whine of decelerating engines filled her ears, she opened her eyes. Around her, she saw the other women perched on the edges of their cots, staring hopefully at the door to their compartment.

They were excited, but afraid to show it. She felt the same.

She hoped they weren't all going to be disappointed.

A sudden jolt announced their arrival. As abruptly as it had begun, the noise of deceleration ceased. The silence was nearly deafening.

Too nervous to stay still any longer, Dalia struggled off of her cot and began pacing the compartment, listening to the sounds of doors banging open and closed around the ship. Finally, she heard the tramp of approaching footsteps and the door to the compartment swung open. Everyone simply stared at the cyborg standing in the entrance, wanting desperately to stampede the door and afraid if they did he'd slam it shut again.

He motioned for them to follow him. Exchanging glances, they surged to their feet almost as one and moved quickly toward the door. Dalia, the only one already on her feet, was the last to reach it. When she stepped into the corridor, she saw it was crowded as the men disgorged from the compartment before theirs into the corridor. In front of her, she caught a glimpse of Pierce's blond hair as he stepped through the door to the men's compartment.

He glanced in her direction, surveyed the females passing closest and finally plastered himself against the bulkhead, allowing everyone to surge around him as he searched for her. Relief and pleasure washed through her. In the next moment, however, she caught a glimpse of Reuel, standing by the gangway. Unnerved, she ducked her head down as he glanced over the heads of those shuffling toward the door. A sense of panic rushed through her.

She wondered if he was looking for her, and if so, why?

It occurred to her that he might not be, that he might merely be watching to make certain everyone disembarked in an orderly fashion, but it didn't matter. Even if he wasn't looking for her in particular, she would have to pass by him unless he disembarked before she made her way to the door.

When she reached Pierce, she met his easy grin with a look of panic. "I think Reuel may be looking for me," she whispered.

Pierce frowned, glancing quickly around the crowded corridor. Nodding finally, he grasped her hand and allowed her to trail slightly behind and to one side of him. Relieved when she saw that Pierce almost completely blocked her view of everyone around them and assuming the same was true from Reuel's viewpoint, Dalia did her best not to attract attention by appearing conspicuous.

She'd almost made it through the door and onto the gangplank, when a hand clamped onto her tunic, pulling her to a stop. She glanced around, knowing even before she saw him that it was Reuel. He glanced from her startled face to Pierce's, his expression hardening. "We have ... matters to settle between us," he said.

It was apparent she wasn't going to be able to avoid the confrontation she'd been dreading. Finally, she nodded and tugged at her hand until Pierce reluctantly released her. "I'll meet you later," she said to Pierce, smiling up at him to allow him to know she was all right with staying.

He searched her gaze and finally lifted his head and looked directly at Reuel. "I'll wait."

"You won't," Reuel said grimly.

Dalia glanced from one man to the other nervously. "It's all right, Pierce. Really. I need to talk to him about ... about his baby."

The comment brought two piercing gazes upon her. She glanced from one man to the other, feeling a sinking sensation in her stomach when she saw that both were incensed. Finally, Pierce nodded and strode down the gangplank. Dalia followed his angry departure with her gaze, glancing blindly at the scene of chaos below as the passengers and crew of the ship collided with the cyborgs that had come to welcome the ship, and finally, reluctantly, turned to Reuel.

"Who is he?" Reuel demanded tightly.

Dalia tilted her head to one side, studying him. "A dear friend," she finally said.

Something flickered in his eyes. He lifted his head, watching Pierce until he disappeared into the crowd below.

Dalia didn't really like the look on his face, or the way he watched Pierce. A shiver skated along her spine. "What do you mean to do with me?"

As she'd hoped, the question brought his attention back to her. He considered her for several moments, glanced around the corridor and gangplank as if he was looking for something and finally caught her upper arm and led her down the corridor in the opposite direction from which she'd come. Finally, he stopped before a door and pushed it open, indicating that she should enter.

She glanced inside, saw that it must be his cabin and looked at him uncomfortably. "I'm fine standing."

His lips tightened. "I'm not."

She debated for a moment and finally stepped inside. When he'd followed her, he closed the door. She moved across the room to a chair, but instead of sitting, she turned to face him. She saw that he'd propped a hip on the top of his desk and was watching her. His gaze flickered over the rounded mound of her belly and finally returned to her face.

"Thirty to forty days," she said.

His brows rose questioningly.

"You were wondering about the ... your infant."

He looked at her piercingly. "Ours."

Confused, Dalia tilted her head curiously. "I don't ... oh!" She shrugged. "I prefer not to think of it that way."

Something flickered in his eyes that made her heart jolt uncomfortably in her chest, but he looked away and she wondered if she had misinterpreted it.

"Why?"

She let out a shaky breath and stared down at the mound that prevented her from looking at her feet. "I don't really want to talk about it."

He scrubbed his hand over his face tiredly. "Why didn't you come to me and tell me about the problem with the female, Zenia?"

Dalia glanced up at him in surprise. "I didn't think about it. I didn't know how even if I had."

He made a sound of frustration and got up from the desk abruptly. "Damn it, Dalia! You could have spoken to the guards. Don't you know I would've done something sooner if I'd known?"

She shrugged. "No, I didn't, but it doesn't matter now, does it?"

"It matters."

She sighed. "I didn't think about it at first. I had no idea it would take so long to get here, or that the infant would grow so fast, or that Zenia would only become more hostile with time instead of less. After a while, I realized she was only awaiting an opportunity to strike. I didn't know what you might do to me if I was embroiled in a fight and the infant was hurt. After a while, I realized I couldn't defend myself anyway. I'd gotten too slow, too clumsy and too weak." She shook her head. "I didn't think any of the others would help me, because they would expect me to be able to defend myself, but then I remembered Pierce from the academy and I knew he would take care of me."

"The blond one."

She looked at him. It wasn't really a question and in any case he knew very well who Pierce was. "What did you do with Zenia?"

He shrugged. "She is being treated. It seems doubtful that her mind can be repaired, but there is nothing we can do but try."

Dalia nodded. She was relieved, not because she particularly cared about Zenia herself, but because she was glad to know that she hadn't misjudged the cyborgs. They might not be human, but they were capable of humane treatment. "What will you do with me when this is finished?" she asked, gesturing toward her abdomen.

He said nothing for several moments and finally Dalia glanced up at him. The pain she'd thought she glimpsed before was evident now and he made no attempt to hide it. "Do you hate me so much?"

Dalia was startled. "I don't hate you at all."

He searched her face and some of the anguish left his expression. "I'm ... as defective in my own way as Zenia," he said at last. "I made mistakes and because I was angry, I made more mistakes, until I didn't know how to make it stop.

"Then, when I saw you with ... him, I knew it was too late and I'd completely screwed everything up."

Dismay filled her. "Don't." She smiled wryly. "We're all defective, I guess. I've made so many mistakes, but I'm learning. I think, I hope, next time, if there is a next time, I'll do better. But I don't hate you because I know you were right. I thought about it a lot. I know what I did was unforgivable. I can't even forgive myself. I wouldn't expect you to. And it was more than that. I was programmed to fight, to kill, not to nurture. I don't think I can. Maybe, in time, I'll change."

He swallowed with an obvious effort. "I didn't mean the things I said to you."

She nodded. "It's all right. I'm over it now."

"Are you?"

She chewed her lip. "Mostly."

"Mostly?" he said pensively, taking a step toward her. "Not completely?"

Dalia eyed him nervously and glanced toward the door. She could see that he'd locked it. She held up her hand. "Don't. Let's just leave it at that."

"I can't."

"Why not?" she said plaintively.

"You know why."

"You don't love me," Dalia said a little desperately, taking another step toward the door to put some space between them. "You couldn't love me and hurt me like that. You couldn't love me and not forgive me."

"How do you know?" he asked quietly, following her step for step.

"Because ... I just do. I know that when you love someone you don't expect them to be perfect and you love them in spite of their mistakes."

He shrugged. "I don't know. I never had love before. I never felt love before. You'll have to teach me." He braced his hands on either side of her head as she flattened herself against the door, unable to open it.

Chapter Seventeen

Reuel bent his head, kissing her cheek when she twisted her face away, then nuzzling her ear. "How is it that you understand it so much better than I, little flower?" he whispered huskily, tugging at her earlobe with his lips.

A shiver of sensation skated over Dalia's flesh. Warmth followed it and a dizzying weakness that made it necessary to lock her wobbly knees. She swallowed. "I'm so horribly swollen. How could you want me, now?"

He pulled away from her and looked down at the huge bulge that kept them apart. Lifting one hand, he skated it lightly over her distended abdomen, as if testing the circumference. When he looked up and met her gaze once more, his eyes glowed with passion. "You are as beautiful to me as you were when I first saw you. This only makes you more beautiful to me, more desirable, not less."

She was more inclined to believe he was too desperate to join his body with hers to care, but she felt much the same. This time when he lowered his lips to hers, she tilted her head up to meet him. Heat seared her as his lips met and clung to her own once, twice. Then he brushed his lips lightly across the sensitive surface of her lips in a tentative caress, as if he was testing his welcome. She inhaled sharply, sucking his breath into her, tasting him on her tongue. The effect was far more devastating to her senses than she remembered. Sighing in defeat, she lifted her hands to his chest and skated her palms upward, clutching his shoulders.

It was all the encouragement he needed. Groaning, he covered her mouth with his own and thrust his tongue inside her to explore her intimately. Another rush of stinging pleasure sparked along her nerve endings. Her skin flushed with sensation.

Her belly clenched painfully with long denied desire.

The baby kicked reflexively.

Reuel jumped back as if he'd been scalded. He stared down at her stomach with such a look of stunned surprise that Dalia burst out laughing.

He glanced at her and slowly a grin dawned. He placed his hand on her stomach tentatively. Sensing the pressure, the baby kicked again. "I felt him."

Dalia laughed. "I'd have been more surprised if you hadn't."

After a moment, he slipped a hand behind her back, bent and put his other arm beneath her knees, and lifted her up. Turning, he strode across the room and set her on her feet beside the bed. Without a word, he caught hold of her gown and pulled it off over her head. Dalia covered her stomach self-consciously, but he pushed her hands away, skimming his own hands over her belly.

Dalia sighed, feeling the heat of burgeoning desire slowly dissipate.

He glanced at her and a slow smile dawned. "This will require some experimentation."

She felt a rush of pleasure. "Will it?"

Stripping his tunic off, he tossed it, grasped her, and climbed into the bed with her. Pushing her flat against the mattress, he levered himself over her and covered her mouth in a kiss that spoke of a hunger that matched or surpassed her own. Instantly, she lost awareness of everything but the feel of his mouth on hers, his taste, the scent of his flesh. The heat that had scarcely waned, surged back tenfold as she stroked his chest, his back, his arms, relishing the feel of his bare flesh. He skated his hands over her in a restless caress of his own, massaging her swollen breasts and distended nipples, caressing her belly and thighs.

When at last he broke the kiss, it was only to follow the path of his hands, to caress her already sensitive flesh with the heat of his mouth. She had missed his kisses most of all, she thought as she watched him moving along her flesh. Whatever he said, whatever he did, he loved her with each hungry kiss, adored her, and it made every touch, every kiss, exquisite, profoundly satisfying. "Tell me you love me," he whispered hoarsely.

She kissed his shoulder, slid a hand along his hard belly, searching for the distended flesh she could feel digging into her thigh. He shifted upward and it skated along her palm, a heated, throbbing, hard length of flesh that filled her hand and made her heart labor even harder, made her lungs struggle to drag air into her chest. Closing her hand around his erection, she stroked him, nipping love bites along the bulging muscles of his upper chest. He groaned, surging against her clenched hand as he sought her lips once more. "Say it," he murmured against her lips before he covered her mouth with his own, kissing her deeply.

Abruptly, he tore his mouth from hers and rolled, carrying her with him until she was straddling his belly. She looked down at him in surprise. He placed his hands along her thighs and surged upwards and she felt his cock slipping along her cleft. "Say it."

She gasped, closing her eyes and focusing on the luscious feel of his hard flesh, relishing the heat and length and breadth of it.

When she opened her eyes to look at him once more, she saw that he'd tucked an arm behind his head, lifting his shoulders off the bed so that he could watch her. Her mouth went dry, moisture and heat flooded her sex with anticipation. Holding her gaze, he looked down at the place where their bodies met. She followed, rising up slightly at his urging and watching as he reached for his cock and rubbed the head of it along her cleft, nudging that place where she desperately wanted him teasingly.

"You love me."

She nodded dizzily, rotating her hips in an effort to fit their bodies together.

"I need to hear you say it," he ground out.

Dalia opened her eyes to look at him as she felt him push the head of his cock past the mouth of her opening. "I love you."

His features went taut. He swallowed convulsively, his gaze searching her face. She smiled, lifting her hand to stroke his cheek. "I do love you."

His eyes slid closed. Groaning, he thrust upward.

She gasped with pleasure as she felt the muscles of her passage yielding to him, pushing back to encompass him completely, until she could feel him nudging against her womb. He caught her hips, urging her to rise up. She lifted, watching his face as he studied the joining of their bodies intently.

They teased each other unhurriedly, holding their rising passions at bay mercilessly, watching the ecstasy flicker across each other's expression. The time came, however, when Dalia knew she couldn't contain it any more. She reached between them, massaging the nub of her clit. Reuel went still, watching her, holding his breath.

Abruptly, he sat up, catching one distended nipple in his mouth and suckling it so hard Dalia's climax struck her shatteringly. She cried out, moving faster now, feeling it rip through her in a scalding flash of heat. He nuzzled her breasts, caught her hips, and forced her to move faster until his own body convulsed in exquisite pleasure, holding her so tightly to him she could scarcely breathe.

Almost reluctantly, he loosened his hold after a few moments. Dragging her down to lie beside him, he stroked the damp hair from her cheeks. "I want...." He paused, as if he was uncertain of how to continue. "I want a family unit."

Dalia swam upwards from near oblivion in surprise. "What?"

His gaze flickered over her face speculatively, doubt surfacing in his eyes. "Will you contract with me?"

Fear surged through her. Dalia sat up abruptly. "I can't. I don't think I can do that."

Reuel sat up, as well, his face a mixture of confusion and anger. "Why?"

"I've no skills ... for that."

He frowned. "You could learn."

"You're angry with me. You would always be angry with me, because I'd make mistakes and ... you don't know how to forgive."

He caught her face between his palms, forcing her to meet his gaze. There was desperation in his eyes, pain. "Teach me," he said earnestly.

Dalia studied his face and finally sighed. "I thought you meant to send me away, to take the baby. I've spent months trying to accept it. I've spent months trying *not* to love you anymore, because I didn't think you loved me. Before, I thought it was what I wanted, anything that you wanted. I can't think now."

He swallowed convulsively and finally pulled her close, tucking her head against his shoulder. "We must start again, from the beginning."

Dalia sighed. "That's just it. I'm not sure I want to again. I tried to tell you."

His arms tightened. "If you hadn't wanted to, if you had stopped caring for me, what just happened between us wouldn't have happened at all, and certainly not as it did."

She said nothing for several moments. Finally, she chuckled. "Do you ever tire of being right?"

He pulled away from her, studied her searchingly and finally smiled faintly as he stroked her cheek. "Not nearly as much as I tire of being wrong. Get dressed. I want to show you your new home."

Dalia felt a surge of both relief and excitement.

Both deflated as she pulled her shift on.

Pierce would almost certainly be waiting and watching for her. "I forgot about Pierce," she muttered.

Reuel's head snapped up. Frowning, he returned his attention to dressing. "You care for him?"

She studied him, realizing he was containing his anger with an effort. It irritated her. "Yes, I do. Too much to want to hurt him."

He studied her speculatively for several moments. "I will show you both your new home," he managed finally.

Dalia turned her face away, biting her lip to keep from smiling. "Is it beautiful?"

He relaxed fractionally. "It is."

She'd more than half hoped she'd been wrong about Pierce when she saw that the crowd that had been below some twenty minutes earlier had vanished, but she saw as they walked down the gangplank that she hadn't been. The moment they started down, Pierce stood away from the column he'd been leaning against. His gaze scanned her briefly, and then zeroed in on Reuel.

Dalia's heart sank. She forced a smile, glancing at the structure at the edge of the landing platform, and then up at the sky and the landscape as far as she could see.

The building had been erected of stone, and built for beauty as well as function. The column Pierce had been leaning on was one of twelve. Each looked to be nearly fifteen feet in height and perhaps three in diameter. At the tops, which supported the roof of the structure, long, broad leaves of had been carved into the stone.

The light of a bright yellow sun shone down upon it, illuminating the interior of the building through tall, wide doors and windows, splashing across a floor paved with colored stones.

Beyond the structure to the east, a young city budded from a flat, green plane.

The air was clean and sweet, the sky bright turquoise.

"It *is* beautiful!" Dalia exclaimed, turning to encompass Reuel with her smile of appreciation.

Pierce's face was taut when they reached him. With an effort, he disengaged his gaze from Reuel's challenging one and looked down at her. "If you don't need me, I should go, I think," he said stiffly.

Dalia grasped his hand, stopping him. Shaking her head ever so slightly, she smiled at him coaxingly. "Reuel offered to show us the city. You're not going to run off?"

Pierce glanced from her hopeful face to Reuel's unwelcoming one. Finally, grinning, he looped his arm through hers. "It doesn't look like a complicated layout. I expect we can find our own way around."

Reuel's eyes narrowed. Matching his pace to theirs, he caught Dalia's other hand and looped it through his arm.

The two men exchanged challenging glances above her head.

Dalia tugged at both of them. "What is this building? I've never seen anything like it."

Smiling in a faintly triumphant way, Reuel glanced down at her. "I designed it after an ancient human structure. I made some modifications, naturally."

"I couldn't help but notice you have a ... passion for ancient things."

Reuel sent her a smoldering glance. "I have a passion for beautiful things."

She could hear Pierce grinding his teeth. "It doesn't look very practical. I'd think it would take a great deal of energy to keep this comfortable. It wouldn't meet the conservation laws of the confederation."

"Human laws do not apply to us. In any case, it is very efficient. It uses virtually no energy to maintain the comfort level because this area we chose to build our city has very little fluctuation in temperatures throughout the year. We wanted to build a city that was beautiful and preserve the natural beauty of our world at the same time, not despoil it as the humans did theirs. Every effort has been made to incorporate the latest conservation technology, because it is wiser to do so than wait until there is no choice."

Dalia sighed with a touch of impatience as they strolled through the structure and out the other side. It seemed likely that Reuel and Pierce would be snipping at one another throughout the tour, but she decided she wasn't going to choose between them and hurt one to please the other, or allow them to spoil her enjoyment.

Determinedly, she forged onward as they left the building and started along the stone paved road that led to the city. She began to tire, however, long before they reached the outskirts, the muscles in her distended belly straining from the walk. Tugging her hands free, she slipped one beneath the weight to support it, rubbing her aching muscles absently with the other.

Chapter Eighteen

"What's wrong?" Reuel and Pierce demanded in stereo.

"Nothing!" she said irritably, struggling to maintain an even breath and wondering why she felt as if she were climbing when the road seemed perfectly flat.

Reuel stopped, glancing from the building they'd just left to the city. "You're tired?" he asked, disbelief evident in his voice.

Dalia gave him a narrow eyed glare. "Try strapping twenty pounds to your cock and carrying it around!" she snapped.

Pierce let out a bark of laughter before he apparently thought better of it. She sent him an evil look. He lifted his brows, assuming a carefully neutral expression. When she glanced back at Reuel, she saw his lips were twitching on the verge of a smile. Quite suddenly, despite the throbbing ache in her back and stomach, Dalia chuckled. "Sorry. It hurts, damn it."

Without a word, Reuel scooped her into his arms.

Pierce glared at both of them, but Dalia found she was too relieved to be off her feet to worry about the prick to his ego at the moment. "I don't suppose there's any ground transportation?" he said tightly.

Reuel glanced at him. "I have personal transport," he said slowly. "But it's across the city, at my home."

"Not very helpful. Why don't you let me take her and you go get the transport?"

Reuel's face darkened. "I can carry her."

"She'd be more comfortable in on a padded seat, though, wouldn't you?"

Dalia glared at both of them. "It would serve you both right if I dropped this thing right here!"

A look of horror washed across both men's faces as they looked at each other sharply. "Majia's balls! You're not going to, though, right?" Pierce exclaimed.

"Now?" Reuel demanded, twisting around and glancing from the building they'd just left to the city once more, realizing it looked much further away than he'd thought.

Until she'd said it, it hadn't occurred to Dalia that there was even a possibility of it. The pain had not really subsided, however, when Reuel had picked her up, and she realized that she'd been struggling to ignore the pain in her back and belly for some time.

Reuel had effectively distracted her for a while, but almost as soon as she'd begun walking it had returned, rapidly becoming much worse that before.

Frowning, she activated her inboard computer. *Computer, analyze the pain radiating from my back through my abdomen.*

Contractions.

What kind of contractions? Dalia asked uneasily, wondering if she shouldn't have made love to Reuel after all.

Birth contractions. The skull of the unknown life-form has been engaged in the pubic cavity. Descending canal.

Dalia felt the blood leave her face. *Can you scan the life-form, computer?*

Scanning. Carbon based life-form. Humanoid.

Stage of development? Dalia asked fearfully. *Can you ascertain whether or not the life-form can survive without the assistance of the host life-form?*

Calculated stage of development, 90%. Internal organ development sufficient to sustain life-form.

If it's only 90%, why is it being born now?

Unknown.

Should it be stopped? Can it be stopped?

Negative.

She looked up at Reuel fearfully, then at Pierce, swallowing with an effort against the lump of anxiety knotting her throat. She licked her lips. "Now."

The single word was sufficient to strike terror in the hearts of both men. They froze, staring at one another as if each one expected the other to come up with a solution. Abruptly, Reuel turned and started walking quickly toward the city.

Pierce fell into step beside them. "Where's the med center?"

"The center of the city," Reuel said grimly.

"How long?"

"Fifteen minutes." He glanced down at Dalia. "Maybe twenty."

"Here, I'll carry her a while."

"No."

"Do you mind?" Dalia demanded, gritting her teeth.

Pierce switched sides. Moving around Reuel, he reached up to stroke her hair back from her face. "Sorry, Dally," he murmured, ignoring the glare Reuel bent on him. "Is it bad?"

"No," she gasped, and then groaned as the pain intensified suddenly. "Yes!"

Reuel walked a little faster.

Dalia panted. "Stop!"

Reuel stopped as if he'd hit a brick wall. "What?"

"This makes my back hurt worse. Put me down. I'll walk a little."

Again, the two men exchanged panicked glances.

"Will you stop it!" she snapped irritably.

Reluctantly, Reuel set her on her feet. Grasping her stomach, Dalia managed a half a dozen shuffling steps before she bent double. "Son of a bitch!" she yelped.

Pierce caught hold of Reuel's wrist, tightening his grip when Reuel would have pulled free. "We'll make a chair for you, baby. Put one arm around his neck and one around mine."

Dalia nodded, hobbling over to them and sitting carefully on their joined arms.

"Better?"

Gritting her teeth, she nodded. She didn't have the heart to tell him that sitting up only made her belly hurt much,

much worse. She dropped her head on Pierce's shoulder, trying to concentrate on filtering out the pain. She could handle it. She knew she could.

She had to. If she scared either one of them any worse, they were liable to drop her and flee.

Once the reached the edge of the city, they gathered a crowd. "What is it? What's wrong with her?" someone questioned them sharply.

"She's having a baby," Pierce snapped.

"What?"

"She's the one?"

"Get the hell out of the way," Reuel growled.

"She's having a baby? It can't be a baby, can it?"

"Of course it's a baby! What the hell else would it be?"

"Cyborg?"

"It's still a baby, fool!"

Dalia's head swam. "Go away," she said faintly.

They didn't. The growing crowd followed them every step of the way until the threesome reached the med center. The word apparently having spread, more rushed up as they went until they had to fight their way through the gathering throng.

At long last, they reached the med center. Reuel grabbed Dalia from Pierce and rushed inside, Pierce on his heels. The moment Pierce cleared the door, he slammed it shut and locked it.

There were five techs in the waiting and treatment area. They stopped, lifting their heads like deer that had caught the scent of the hunter. Five pairs of eyes zeroed in on her bulging belly.

"She needs ... something," Reuel growled. "The baby's coming."

The med techs merely stared at him blankly. "You mean birth?" one of them finally said.

"Yes!" Pierce snapped. "Birth. Now!"

"But ... she's not supposed to now. They told me it would be months."

Dalia groaned, demanding to be put down and Reuel set her carefully on her feet, supporting her with an arm around her waist. Her feet had no sooner touched the tile floor than something hot and wet rushed between her thighs, running down her legs and forming a puddle on the floor. Dalia gasped fearfully. "What is that? What's happening?"

"Urine?" the med tech nearest her guessed.

Dalia glared at him and slapped him square across the jaw. "It's *something* from the baby!"

Abruptly, all five med techs sprang into action, launching themselves in five different directions at once. Unfortunately, their paths converged. They slammed together with a noise like a clap of thunder. One of the females bounced backward, slammed into the wall and then hit the floor on her hands and knees. Before she could gain her feet, two of the other three fell over her.

"You were supposed to be ready!" Reuel roared furiously.

Wordlessly, the med techs scrambled to their feet and rushed away. In a few moments, one came barreling down the corridor pushing a gurney in front of him. As he slid to a stop in front of Reuel and Dalia, another med tech rushed up with some sort of monitoring device on wheels. When Reuel had lifted her and settled her on the gurney, they turned and went back down the corridor to an examination room.

Reuel and Pierce exchanged a long look and followed. Taking up position on either side of the door, they folded their arms, leaned back against the wall, and watched the proceedings suspiciously.

Pierce glanced at Reuel. "Do they know what they're doing?"

"They damn well better," Reuel growled, but he didn't like the way the med techs kept exchanging nervous glances. Finally, one of the techs dashed past them and out the door. Ten minutes later, he returned with an antiquated computer on wheels, pushed it across the room, and hooked it up.

Reuel covered his face with his hands when they pulled up an even more ancient, pictorial medical encyclopedia and began clicking through the pages frantically. By the time they'd found the passages they needed and began a checklist, Dalia looked and sounded as if she was dying, her panting gasps escaping more like hoarse screams of agony.

White-faced, Reuel stood away from the wall abruptly and left the room.

Pierce stayed, watching as one of the med techs moved to the foot of the gurney, pushed Dalia's legs up until her knees were almost perpendicular and parted her thighs. After leaning close and studying her for several moments, he poked his head up again and looked at the computer screen. "What did it say it was supposed to look like?"

The question was bad enough. One glimpse of the round black blob protruding from her body and the blood trickling out around sent a wave of dizziness through him. With an effort, he felt his way blindly out the door, slid down the wall and put his head down.

Reuel stopped pacing, staring down at Pierce in abject terror. "What's wrong?"

"Everything, I think," Pierce said a little sickly. "When you were checking out this natural reproduction thing, did you happen to check to see if many of the females survived it?"

Feeling the blood rush from his face, Reuel thrust the door open and reentered the examination room just in time to see a horrible, bloody mass slither from Dalia's body and into the waiting hands of one of the techs. He knew then that Pierce was right. Dalia was dying and the infant he'd looked forward to with so much hope was nothing more than a bloody mass of biological material that looked as if it had gone through a defective particle transporter. Blackness swarmed around him. His knees suddenly felt like jelly. He felt himself sway.

The next moment he was aware of, he was staring up at the ceiling and listening to a weak, strange noise that sounded like a combination of crying and choking.

Confused, both by that and the fact that his skull felt as if he'd cracked it open, he sat up slowly, holding his pounding head and trying to figure out how he'd gotten back into the corridor when he didn't remember leaving the examination room.

"Hey!" Pierce exclaimed, chuckling. "It looks like a baby!"

Hope surging through him at that announcement, Reuel struggled to his feet with an effort, reentered the examination room, and shoved Pierce aside. Relief flooded him as he watched one of the techs carefully wiping the bloody residue off of the screaming child. He could tell nothing about the face, beyond the fact that the mouth worked. It was wide open. There were slits where the eyes were supposed to be. He sincerely hoped that only meant that it had squeezed them closed. It was red with fury and waving two arms and two legs, with two hands and two feet. He counted ten fingers and ten toes. It was definitely humanoid. A slow smile curled his lips. "It's a female."

Dalia chuckled weakly and reached for the squalling infant. It began to grow quieter almost at once and Reuel moved to the head of the gurney, smiling as he watched it wiggle around in search of a comfortable position. Finally, it managed to get one of its waving fingers in its mouth and began sucking. Dalia flicked a look up at his face. "I'm all right, thanks," she said dryly.

Reuel flushed uncomfortably. Catching her hand, he lifted it to his lips and kissed the back and then leaned down and kissed her lips. "You're wrong if you think I wasn't worried. I've never been that scared before in my life. I'm just so ... overwhelmed."

"Guess that's why you fainted?" Pierce commented. At the withering glance Reuel sent in his direction, he added, "I'd say that probably makes it unanimous." He turned to study the departing med techs. "They need reprogramming."

Reuel gave him a look. "We'll all need some. We've got nearly six thousand cyborgs on Mordal and three thousand in the city Gallen, most of whom were designed as soldiers and damn few with any other kind of training." He gestured toward the group that had just left. "They were programmed as med techs for battle wounds, not medical conditions, sickness, and most definitely not for delivering babies."

Pierce shrugged. "Guess that's why they didn't know their ass from a hole in the ground?" He transferred his attention to Dalia and the infant. "Anyway, you've got a beautiful baby, Dally."

Dalia looked at the baby a little doubtfully. "You think so?"

"No."

Dalia glared at him. "If you had any idea of the hell I just went through, you'd lie."

Pierce sobered. "I've got a pretty good idea--and I was just teasing you. She's strong, healthy and got everything she's supposed to have. That makes her beautiful."

Dalia shifted the baby so that she could study its sleeping face. A smile tugged at her lips. "She looks like Reuel."

"Really? No wonder she's ugly as hell. Poor little tyke."

Dalia chuckled at the look on Reuel's face. It was obvious he didn't know whether to be more insulted by her remark or Pierce's. Before he could think up a suitable retort, a great roar filtered through the building to them.

"What was that?" Dalia asked uneasily.

Reuel and Pierce exchanged a glance and left the room. Pierce was grinning when they returned and Reuel looking very pleased with himself. "They're celebrating," Reuel said, his voice threaded with pride and excitement, "the birth of the first cyborg."

"The birth of the first child born on Mordal," Pierce added.

"I should take her and show them," Reuel said, studying the infant a little doubtfully.

Dalia gave him a look. "Don't even think about it. The computer said she was only 90% matured. They can see her when she's a little older."

"Yeah," Pierce added. "Hopefully, she'll look better, too.... What?" he added when Reuel and Dalia both gave him an indignant glare.

Chapter Nineteen

Dalia was overwhelmed when they left the med center two days later. Hundreds of cyborgs, both male and female, lined the walks on either side of the street, trying to get a glimpse of the infant, cheering almost hysterically each time she lifted it up for them to see it.

Reuel, despite his suggestion of taking it out to show the day it was born, wasn't terribly anxious to hold it. He seemed perfectly content to stare at her for hours, but every time she handed the infant to him, he went rigid, hardly daring even to breathe. That was usually followed by a sickly, greenish pallor to his skin and a cold sweat.

Pierce didn't do much better. As long as he wasn't holding the infant, he was completely nonchalant about the care of it, and eager to impart the wisdom of infant care that he 'remembered' from his childhood programming. The moment she suggested he hold it, however, he thought of something else he had to do and disappeared.

She couldn't say that she blamed them. She was terrified of it herself. She hadn't expected it to be so tiny, or look so fragile and helpless. It couldn't even feed itself, let alone look for its own food. And it almost seemed as if, when she did feed it the liquid diet the med techs assured her were all the sustenance it needed right now, the food poured right through it and out the other end. It was constantly soiling itself, which was another reason neither Reuel nor Pierce wanted to hold it.

She hadn't wanted to voice her fears aloud, but she couldn't help but worry that something was very wrong.

The new residents of the cyborg world had been assigned to the homes of those who'd come before them until they decided to stay and build their own abode or leave. And Dalia discovered that she was to make her home with Reuel, which didn't surprise her. What did was that Reuel had arranged to take Pierce, as well, until it occurred to her that Pierce was one of the minute few who had any prior knowledge of infants.

Reuel's abode, or 'home' as he referred to it, was what he called a 'plantation' about a mile beyond the outer rim of the city of Gallen. He grew food, but also plants that were used to make other things.

She'd been surprised to learn of it, until it occurred to her that they would have to have something like it to provide a continuous supply of food. It had taken them three months to get to Mordal. Even if it hadn't been dangerous to regularly travel between the planet and others for supplies, it wasn't practical.

Then, too, Mordal had no monetary system like the known universe. The cyborgs traded for what they wanted. The fact that Reuel grew food and everyone needed food meant that Reuel was one of the wealthiest cyborgs on the planet, particularly since he also seemed to understand the techniques of growing better than anyone else and produced far more than any of the other planters.

His abode was startling even after all of the other buildings Dalia had seen since she'd arrived. For one thing, it was an enormous structure of many rooms. On Earth, one was fortunate even to have soul possession and use of one large room. Reuel's house had ten rooms of staggering proportions. Even the rooms for bathing were larger than the quarters she'd had. Most of the storage compartments were larger than her quarters.

He was obviously fond of what he referred to as porches, which were, basically, rooms on the outside of the building that had a floor and ceiling, but no walls or windows beyond those that made up the outer wall of the house--and columns. A porch ran the width of the building on the front and was lined with tall columns that supported the outer edge of the roof. These columns were not smooth like those at the flight terminal, however. They had regular, concave gouges running vertically around their circumference, which Reuel referred to as fluting. The decorative tops of the columns were also more elaborately carved.

Kaitlyn O'Connor

It had windows everywhere, most of them tall enough they could've been doors if they'd been set nearer the floor. The doors were big enough for giants.

Staring at the enormous white structure as they neared it, Dalia felt her stomach go weightless. She wasn't certain whether it was the beauty of the building itself that inspired such awe, or if that was only part of it, but she was aware of equal parts of admiration and gut wrenching fear--of so much space and of occupying it with Reuel.

He hadn't said anything else about contracting as a family unit, but she was fairly certain that wasn't because he'd forgotten it or dismissed the idea. She had the distinct feeling that he thought she would grow accustomed to it by sharing his abode with him and the infant.

She wasn't certain she would. She hadn't experienced anything since the birth of the infant to convince her she'd been wrong about not having nurturing instincts. The infant seemed to trust her, which only proved the poor thing hadn't developed adequate logic capabilities, because she hadn't a clue of what she was doing, or if she was doing any of it correctly. The only reason she hadn't handed it to Reuel and fled was because he wouldn't take it long enough, she didn't think the city of Gallen was large enough for her to hide, and she hated for everyone to know how incompetent she was.

Since the techs had insisted that she must refrain from sexual activities for at least a few weeks due to the condition of her body from the birth, Reuel settled her in a room by herself ... well, almost. He had set the room up with a tiny bed that had sides for the infant. She would've rather he'd put the infant in another room, but, she supposed since the food went through it before it had time to assimilate much of it, it had to be fed every few hours to keep it from starving to death. And, for some reason, Reuel and Pierce, who never agreed on anything else, decided she was best qualified for that job.

She decided to accept the decision without argument--for the time being. She fully intended to see to it that she wasn't saddled with the entire responsibility of nurturing, however. Reuel had contributed, and he could damn well accept that he was going to be sharing the responsibility of parenting. For that matter, she saw no reason for Pierce not to if he was going to continue living at the plantation for a while.

Despite that resolve, she resented the fact that their idea of 'helping' was to leave the house altogether so that they wouldn't accidentally wake the infant, especially when she wanted to do nothing but sleep and she was only allowed a few hours at a stretch. But she found that it was oddly satisfying to cuddle the tiny thing and hold the bottle while it drank.

It had developed the habit of clutching a fistful of her tunic while she held it. She didn't know whether that meant it sensed she might drop it and didn't fully trust her, or if it was just trying to stay close to her because it had been attached inside of her so long and thought it was still supposed to be attached.

"We should name it," she announced to Reuel and Pierce once they'd settled into their rooms and gathered in the 'small' informal living area that adjoined the bedrooms, which were all on the second floor of the house.

Reuel smiled faintly, glancing around the room with obvious pride. "I did. I call it Tara, from one of the ancient paper books I've collected."

Following his gaze, Dalia rolled her eyes. "The infant!"

"Oh." Reuel looked at her sheepishly.

"Reuela?" Pierce suggested.

Dalia looked at him suspiciously. "Reuela?" she echoed.

He shrugged. "You said it looked like Reuel. I don't see it myself, but she does have black hair like his."

"My moth..." Dalia stopped self-consciously. After a moment, she cleared her throat and started over. "My mother's second name was Claire."

Reuel studied her, his expression unreadable. "Then we'll name her Claire," he said finally, then turned and left the room.

Pierce's eyebrows rose. "What's his problem, you think?"

Dalia sighed. "I think its because he doesn't have memories like we do. Of course, we know now they were only planted, but ... even knowing it, I still feel like it happened. He ... none of the cyborgs have that. I think there's just sort of an emptiness, a feeling that they missed something important. They don't have a ... history. I think, maybe, that's one of the reasons Reuel is so fascinated with historical things."

Pierce frowned. "They've done a hell of a job building this place. Why don't they just program it in like we were programmed?"

Dalia shrugged. "Pride, maybe? They don't want to admit they feel inferior in any way? But I don't think they have the technology to do anything like that anyway. You saw the thing the med techs were using. It must have been a hundred years old! *We* were cutting edge, even for the company. Short of taking one of us apart for study, I wouldn't think they'd be able to develop the technology to do it if they wanted to."

* * * *

A week after Dalia had given birth, the four of them were summoned to attend a general meeting of the council at the municipal center to address the state of their tiny nation.

Dalia was nervous. She knew at least a part of the reason for it was to reassure the cyborg community that reproduction among them had been a success, but Claire still couldn't talk. She had begun to actually look much better, but she still looked strangely misshapen to Dalia's mind. She was stronger and she showed signs of developing mental capabilities by looking around her curiously, but Dalia still had the uneasy feeling that she'd somehow fucked up the most momentous assignment she'd ever been given and that the infant wasn't 'normal'.

It was only to be expected that she would be small. She would have to be considering the limited space she had to grow, but shouldn't she be just a smaller version of a full grown female? And, if it were just a lack of maturity, how long would it take before she looked more like she should?

The data banks were still gathering information. The data gathered by her own inboard computer regarding the changes in her body and the development of the fetus had been downloaded into it before she left the med center. She was to take the infant back for weekly scans to gather developmental information and had already taken Claire to her first the day before the meeting, but there simply wasn't enough data yet to make a determination. Until and unless they were able to gather information on more than one subject, they had nothing to compare the data they gathered on Claire against except the information in the computers about human infants.

Physiologically, she was almost identical to a human infant, except for the fact that she contained cyborg DNA and a far higher metal content than found in humans. Her bone structure wasn't titanium as Dalia's and Reuel's were, but it wasn't primarily calcium either, like human bone. It was something with a high titanium content that the computer was unable to identify. Developmentally, the med techs indicated that Claire was maturing at a faster rate than a human infant. That fact seemed to disturb the med techs, who apparently had expected that she would mature at a similar rate. And Dalia went from worrying about Claire being underdeveloped to worrying that she was maturing too fast and then back again when it dawned on her that the med techs hardly seemed to have a clue of what was happening themselves.

And why should they when the entire thing was unprecedented?

The municipal hall was already packed by the time they arrived, but they were shown to seats at the front that had been set aside specifically for them. It continued to fill for another thirty minutes before the president of the colony called for order and stood up to address the assemblage. He looked out over the sea of faces for several moments before he spoke.

"We want to welcome those of you who have just joined us here in Gallen. I am well aware that you were not given a choice, but it was never our intention to deprive you of a choice. Rather, we hoped to gain the chance to make friends of our enemies. Some of you will almost certainly decide that you prefer the world you have known to the one that we are building. We hope that most of you, however, will find a place for yourselves and that, eventually, we will all live together as friends, neighbors and allies and no longer consider ourselves enemies.

"Any of you who feel after spending a year here that you would prefer to leave will be escorted beyond our system to one of the worlds near the outer rim.

"I caution you, however, to consider the matter carefully. Once you have been expelled, you will not be welcomed again for the simple reason that we are in agreement that anyone who cannot adjust in a year cannot adjust at all and would never be a useful citizen."

He paused for questions after the announcement. The question and answer session went on for almost an hour, but he continued to take questions until everyone appeared satisfied that their doubts had been addressed.

Dalia, Reuel and Claire were summoned up onto the platform next to display the infant. A quiet fell over the auditorium that might have been awe or dismay, as everyone stared at the baby. Dalia wasn't certain which, but it unnerved her. Reuel didn't seem to share her reservations. He looked as proud of her as if she'd actually been beautiful and intelligent instead of an odd lump of uncoordinated flesh whose only accomplishments to date were staring around curiously, evacuating its body waste with regularity and screaming every time it was hungry, wet, soiled, tired or just bored.

More accurately, she supposed, he looked as proud as if he'd single-handedly accomplished something no one else had ever accomplished.

An odd sort of warmth filled her as she watched him, however, an odd sense of fulfillment and she realized with a little surprise that it was the other side of sexual love. It was a feeling of being connected to someone else, happy, content, comfortable.

It confused her and troubled her. When they'd returned to their seats, she glanced surreptitiously at Pierce, who sat beside her holding the baby on his lap now.

She'd almost always felt that way, or a lot like that, about Pierce. He'd never stunned her breathless with desire only by looking at her. As attractive as she thought he was, she'd never been tempted to cross the line and defy company law by engaging in sexual activities with him, but he had a way about him that had always made her feel safe just being around him. He made her laugh. It made her feel good, both content and comfortable, just listening to his almost constant banter.

Did she love both of them? Or was it simply that she'd didn't grasp the emotion as she'd thought she did?

The president drew her attention once more and she looked up at him almost with a sense of reprieve from her troubling thoughts.

He looked uncomfortable now and she frowned. She didn't think it had to do with the baby, however, not directly anyway. He'd read out the information they'd gathered after she and Reuel had left the platform and he'd, once more, answered all of the questions put to him. Though, naturally enough, there was still far more they didn't know than they did. He'd managed to convince everyone, however, that Claire was a resounding success, and exactly as had been expected. No one had seemed particularly thrilled about the idea of producing such helpless, underdeveloped creatures and then having to nurture them to maturity, but they seemed content to accept that it was 'normal'.

"We have some serious issues that must be addressed," the president said finally. "Before I announce the new laws that we've passed, I want to assure everyone that these issues were not taken lightly or the decision an easy one. We spent months deliberating and debating and have finally reached what we feel is the solution most beneficial to everyone."

He paused, either to allow that much to sink in or because he was still wrestling with the best way to make an announcement he expected to be taken poorly. "Baby Claire is the first offspring of our kind, but we have great expectations, tremendous hopes, that she will not be the last, that many of us will also be given the chance to found our own bloodlines.

"Those hopes led to the decision to form family units to ensure a stronger bonding of our community members. Our creators have ceased to see the value of family units except on underdeveloped worlds like ours, but their conclusions of the benefits of family units in developing worlds leads us to consider it essential to our own growth.

"The problem arises that we are not just small in numbers, however. A traditional family unit among the humans would consist of a male, a female and offspring, as most of you are aware. We have four times the number of males than females and we cannot even be certain at this point that they will agree to stay. Half the females included in that number are among the newcomers.

"If we allow our community to simply pair off, more than half the males will have no chance of finding a mate or family partner. This is unacceptable, not the least of which because it will almost certainly create a great deal of resentment in half our population, strife, conflict, competition for the available females that could wreck our chances of building what we want.

"The only solution we could come up with that would serve the community is to pass a law prohibiting contracting of family units of pairs. Contracts must be left open to provide for at least one additional male, but not more than four."

Chapter Twenty

The president's hope of heading off an outpouring of outrage by explaining the circumstances before the announcement proved forlorn. The words were hardly out of his mouth before the entire room exploded, half of them jumping to their feet. It took almost thirty minutes to bring order. By the time it had been restored, the president looked as furious as everyone else.

"Considering your displeasure with our solution to our problem, I think it should be clear enough that anything short of that would have been received far more poorly. None of us were completely satisfied. We don't expect you to be completely satisfied. However, it *is* the law. It will be strictly enforced, because it is in the best interests of all.

"I'm sure those of you who have already formed an attachment are more disturbed than others who haven't, but you must consider whether it would be better to accept and adapt, or better to have to constantly guard your female from theft and wage battle against challengers.

"We cannot hope to establish any sort of civilized societal structure under those conditions."

Emotions might be difficult for the cyborg community to handle, but logic was still strong in them. They quieted, settled into their seats once more, and considered the situation while questions were answered. Finally, still displeased, they accepted that the solution had merits, especially since it increased their odds of a mate, even if it was a shared one, substantially.

Dalia wasn't certain how the other females in the group felt, but she wasn't completely comfortable with it. What no one had pointed out was that, even though the solution sounded logical and *was* best for all concerned, the cyborg males were nearly as territorial as their human counterparts, perhaps more so. Many of the females were almost as territorial, which meant that the majority of the battles would be fought in the homes instead of on the streets.

She hadn't dared even glance in Reuel's direction since the announcement. He'd been furious, and he and Pierce had been engaged in a glaring match above her head ever since. If she chose them, and she certainly wouldn't consider choosing anyone else, she would have to be standing between them constantly, at least until they adjusted to the idea, assuming they ever would.

It was almost more tempting to consider leaving the colony and taking her chances with the company. At least in that instance, she would have some peace.

They returned to the plantation in complete silence. Once they reached it, Dalia fled to her room and locked the door. She knew she wasn't going to be able to simply ignore the issue altogether, but she thought it best to allow Reuel time to come to terms with the law itself before there was any discussion on a more personal level.

Remaining single wasn't an option for the females. If they stayed, they were expected to play a pivotal role in establishing family units, not create more conflict by refusing to accept even one male. So, unless she wanted to leave, which she didn't, she couldn't avoid Reuel's displeasure by simply refusing to commit at all.

For a week, everyone seemed determined to avoid everyone else as much as possible. Peace reigned in the household until the second week, when Pierce decided to court her since Reuel didn't seem to be making a push in that direction.

Conflict erupted almost immediately, but it didn't manifest itself in actual violence until the third week, at least as far as Dalia knew. Unfortunately, it appeared to be her effort to prevent that eventuality that provoked it.

They had taken up the practice of spending time in the informal living area in the evenings before bed and continued to even after the competition between Reuel and Pierce reached a point two weeks after the president's announcement that made it uncomfortable.

"We have to establish some house rules," she said resolutely, standing up and addressing both Reuel and Pierce.

Reuel's eyes narrowed. "It's my house. It's my plantation. I make the rules."

Dalia studied him for several moments in tight-lipped silence. Finally, she sighed. "You're right." She glanced at Pierce. "I'm going down to the land office tomorrow to see what's available. Would you mind coming along to help me with Claire?"

Pierce sent Reuel a wicked look and grinned at her. "Sure. I've been thinking about trying my hand at being a planter since I started helping Reuel around here. I think I could be good at it."

Dalia nodded and got up. She stopped on the way to her room and looked back at Reuel. "Actually, Claire's yours, too. I'll just leave her here with you."

She could see Reuel was already furious. Her parting shot pulled the rug out from under him. "I'm willing to hear you out," he said ungraciously.

"That's so magnanimous of you!" she retorted tartly.

He ground his teeth. "Do you want to talk about it or not?" he ground out.

"Not if you don't plan on being reasonable."

"He's a 'borg, Dally. In case you haven't noticed, they're not very reasonable."

Dalia glared at Pierce. Before she could comment on such deliberate provocation, however, Reuel slugged him across the jaw so hard he flew backwards over the couch and skidded across the carpet almost to the wall. The moment he came to a halt, Pierce jumped to his feet with a roar of fury and launched himself toward Reuel, leaping over the couch. Reuel made no attempt to avoid him and Dalia was just thinking that he'd thought better of engaging in a full out battle in the house when, having waited until Pierce was within arm's reach, he executed a lightening fast punch that knocked Pierce's feet out from under him.

Pierce landed on the floor at his feet, flat of his back. He wasn't stunned long, however. Swinging one arm, he clipped the back of Reuel's knees hard enough that Reuel fell backwards.

The baby had merely gaped at the two men in stunned surprise when Reuel had thrown the first punch. When he slugged Pierce the second time, she let out a blood-curdling shriek and kept on screaming. Cuddling her close, Dalia went into their room and slammed the door. It took her nearly thirty minutes to quiet the baby and she discovered that thirty minutes of infant wails were more torturous than anyone unfamiliar with that particular noise could possibly comprehend. It would've been easier, she thought, if not for the grunts, growls, meaty thuds, crashes of furniture and the tinkling sound of breaking glass.

Finally, Reuel and Pierce either reached an understanding, exhausted themselves, or reached unconsciousness. Silence fell and she managed to quiet the baby and get her to sleep. When she did, Dalia went out to assess the damage. The room was a shambles. Pierce was sitting on the floor in the middle of the wreckage, massaging his jaw and grinning at Reuel, who gingerly examining a black eye using a piece of what had once been a three foot square wall mirror but was now in fragments, most of them less than two inches.

Plunking her hands on her hips, Dalia glared at both of them. "Claire is asleep. If either one of you makes a single sound that wakes her up and sets her off again, I swear, I'll kill you myself! I've *changed* my mind! I don't want either damn one of you!"

When she returned from the land office the following day, the room was spotless. The broken furniture had been removed and replaced or repaired. Reuel and Pierce were sitting in chairs on either side of the room, glaring at each other, but the moment she stopped in the doorway they assumed carefully neutral expressions.

Reuel cleared his throat. "I apologize for last night. This is--I'd like for this to be *our* home."

He seemed sincere enough, and the truth was Dalia didn't want to have to choose anyone else, but she wasn't about to contract with anyone who wasn't willing to treat her as a full partner. "You have a real problem with ownership,

Reuel," she said quietly. "That's the main reason I didn't agree to a contract between us before. I think I understand why. And I know it's something you probably can't change, but you'll have to at least make an effort to restrain your possessiveness or find another partner because I will be a full partner in any contract I agree to."

He frowned, but thoughtfully, and finally nodded.

"We'd like to hear the house rules," Pierce said coolly.

Dalia glanced at him. "Good. Up until now I'm the only person here who has done any of the work in taking care of baby Claire. I love her and I don't mind. What I do mind is not being treated as an equal around here. So, the new house rule is that everybody takes a turn tending to baby Claire for however long it takes until she can take care of herself. Before, I didn't know any more about nurturing than either of you. If I can learn, both of you can learn. So, from now on, we rotate, bedtime to bedtime. She goes to sleep at seven."

Reuel flushed. "That's the house rule?"

Dalia gave him a look. "That's the house rule I intended to talk about last night. There's another one tonight. No fighting in the house, period. If you two just have to slug it out, take it outside. It scares Claire."

Pierce and Reuel exchanged a sheepish glance. Pierce cleared his throat uncomfortably. "I hope you didn't mean what you said--about the contract, I mean. I'd considered asking you about it after the president made the announcement, but you didn't seem to want to talk about it."

Dalia blushed. "I made the assumption that you wanted to. I shouldn't have, but I was angry. I wasn't thinking clearly. I can't when Claire's been screaming in my ear for an hour."

"You weren't wrong and I wasn't criticizing. I'm just asking if you'll reconsider."

Dalia turned to look at Reuel. He looked almost as angry as he had the night of the announcement, but he swallowed his spleen with an effort. "I'd just as soon not share you with Pierce or anyone, but the alternative doesn't appeal to me. I suppose if the only choice is being one of two partners, I mean to be one of them--if you'll have me," he added uncomfortably.

Relief flooded her. Dalia smiled tremulously. "I was afraid the two of you would behave so badly I'd have to contract with someone else."

Moving quickly across the room, she leaned over the baby's head and kissed Reuel lightly on the lips. "Yes! I love you!" Before he could grab her, she plopped the baby down in his lap. "It's your night."

He was still gaping at her in dismay when she cut off Pierce's retreat by grabbing hold back of his tunic. "No you don't!"

He turned to look at her, both hurt and anger in his eyes.

Dismay filled her. Ordinarily, even if he'd been hurt he would've tried to pass it off with a joke. "Sit on the porch with me?"

She thought for several moments that he would refuse. Finally, reluctantly, he nodded. She knew Reuel was probably no happier than Pierce, but she could only handle one problem at the time so she ignored the look she knew he'd bent upon. Unfortunately, possibly because she saw that Dalia was leaving without her and she'd become accustomed to being only with Dalia, Claire chose that moment to object, loudly.

"Dalia?" Reuel exclaimed, jumping to his feet.

Sighing, Dalia glanced at Pierce. "I'll meet you on the porch in a few minutes?"

He shrugged. "Sure."

When he'd left, she went back to Reuel, took the baby and then sat down in Reuel's lap. "You're going to have to learn to handle this," she said.

He knew she wasn't referring only to the baby. "I don't honestly know if I can."

She studied his face lovingly. "Nothing is going to change the way I feel about you. Not even you." Turning the baby, she settled her against Reuel's shoulder. "She's not used to you and it'll take time. Walk her and pat her back. Sing to her if you know a song. If that doesn't work, try bouncing her and if that doesn't work try shaking something sparkly in front of her face. I have a bottle all ready for her, and when she's eaten, she'll go right to sleep. But you can't give it to her while she's upset. She'll choke or she just won't take it."

Reuel nodded. When she got up, he stood and started walking the baby. Dalia watched the two of them until she saw the baby had stopped crying and was staring at Reuel in blank-faced amazement and then slipped downstairs.

To her relief, Pierce was standing on the porch, leaning against one of the columns. When he saw her, he pushed away from the column and started pacing the porch. Sighing, she glanced around the porch and finally chose the rocking chair and sat down, rocking as she gazed out at the stars in the sky.

When Pierce finally stopped pacing and halted by her chair, she got up and gestured for him to take it. As soon as he'd settled himself, she climbed onto his lap. "I'm used to Reuel being quiet and not talkative when he's angry. I don't like it, but I've leaned how to deal with it. You're not usually like this, though."

Pierce let out a gusty sigh, as if he'd been holding his breath. "It tears me up, Dally. I don't know if I can handle this. I thought I could if you'd just give me a chance. Hell, I guess if it wasn't for the law I wouldn't have any chance at all. I knew there was something going on between the two of you from the first. I figured he'd probably fathered the baby, but I still, thought, maybe, there was a chance you felt something for me.

"I've been crazy in love with you, Dally, since the first time I saw you. First it was the damn company's laws that kept me away from you, and now this."

Dalia laid her head on his shoulder. "You don't think it's possible to love more than one person?"

Pierce was silent so long she'd begun to wonder if he would say anything at all. "I don't know."

"Humans do."

"No, they don't. Some of them only love themselves, and some of them love someone, but none of them love more than one female or one male at the time."

"So ... what you're saying is you think it's possible, but only one at the time? If you love one person and then begin to love another person, you have to stop loving the first one in order to be able to love the second?"

"I guess. You don't see humans taking on two partners, except when they're cheating on each other."

Dalia sighed. "Maybe I feel this way because I'm not human, then."

Pierce swallowed audibly. "You just told Reuel you loved him. You're saying, now, that you love me?"

Dalia sat up and looked at him. "Don't do that."

"What?"

"Don't compare. If you don't believe me, or you don't want to, or you just can't, then I'll try to understand, but I know what I feel. I sought you out when we were on the ship because I knew you would take care of me, unquestioningly."

He sighed. "I was that obvious."

"No. I thought you might like to be more than friends, but I wasn't sure. I just knew you were my best friend and that I could count on you."

"I don't want to be your friend," he said harshly.

She caressed his cheek. "It would hurt me indescribably if you stopped being my friend. I want you to be my partner, my lover, and my friend. If you chose someone else, I'd die every time I saw you with her."

He frowned. "Well maybe you understand a little better how I feel."

She shook her head. "You're wrong if you think I don't. I understand completely how you feel. What would you have me do?"

He slipped an arm around her shoulders. "We could leave."

"A year from now. I have to choose a partner within the next six months."

He swallowed. "Then choose me, Dally. We can leave before you have to choose another."

"I love Claire. I couldn't leave her."

"We'll take her."

She shook her head and scooted off his lap. "I love Reuel too much to do that to him. Anyway I look at it, I have to hurt somebody that means a lot to me. I'm beginning to wish Reuel had just killed me when he caught me ... or that I hadn't woke up when the tech was about to.

"I'll contract with both you and Reuel. Or I won't contract with either of you."

Chapter Twenty-One

Dalia was absolutely petrified when she, Reuel and Pierce entered the records office and signed a family unit contract. She could well imagine what the clerk thought of it, for both Reuel and Pierce looked more like condemned men at an execution than happy partners.

It was some relief to discover that they were the fourth party to do so. Dalia didn't think she could have handled it if they'd had to endure another 'first' ceremony.

The three of them had finally sat down together and worked up partnership rules they felt like they could live with. Dalia could display her affection for either partner, in any way she chose, at any time, and neither of the other partners could express or display anger either during or afterward. If they didn't like it, they could walk it off, but they were not to deliberately provoke each other either by word or deed in regards to possessiveness or jealousy.

Any disputes arising from any other source, or for any other reason, would be settled however they wanted to settle them, outside, and never within view or hearing of the baby. For Claire, or any other children they were fortunate enough to have, they would present a unified, civil, reasonably content family unit.

The three of them would continue to have their own room. The baby would sleep in the room with whomever was supposed to keep her on any given night until she reached a stage in development where she could have her own room.

Sexual congress between Dalia and her two partners was to be as fair and even as she could make it so that neither of her partners felt as if they were favored above the other.

It sounded workable in theory. Dalia wasn't at all sure it would, but they were about to find out. After the signing, they decided to dine out to celebrate. Claire enjoyed the first thirty minutes and began to fuss as soon as the food arrived. It was Dalia's night to keep her, but, in the spirit of their new partnership, Pierce offered to hold her while Dalia ate.

When they returned home, Dalia looked at both her hopeful partners and smiled apologetically. "Tonight's Claire's night," she said, shrugging. Seeing that both of them were about to object, she added, "I'd rather not be interrupted and have to get up and walk the baby."

Pierce and Reuel exchanged a look. "Cards or chess?" Pierce asked.

Feeling far more hopeful that they might actually manage a comfortable relationship between the three of them, Dalia retreated to the room with the baby. Claire slept for the first time without waking once, but Dalia found she was having a good bit of trouble sleeping. The following day was to be Reuel's day to keep Claire and she found she was both excited and nervous about spending her first night with Pierce.

She tried to dismiss it. It seemed absurd to feel so jittery when she'd always felt so comfortable around him, but it continued to plague her dreams even after she slept and, despite the fact that she was busy the following day, it only got worse as the day wore on.

She supposed, deep down, that she was worried that they might not click as well in bed as they did the rest of the time, and that Pierce would be disappointed in her. Or, perhaps worse, she would find that they weren't sexually compatible and might have trouble convincing Pierce that she found him as desirable as she did Reuel.

Whatever the case, when she finally realized that she, Reuel and Pierce were all watching the clock that evening, she decided to go to her room and try to reach a state of calm. There was a great deal to be said for a hot soak over the perfectly balanced temp of a particle bath. Bathing in water had its own drawbacks, but the soothing power of water could not be underestimated.

She soaked until she heard Reuel leave the living area with the baby. She didn't want her time with Pierce spoiled any more than vice versa and she thought the best way to avoid it was to make certain she didn't run into Reuel on the way to Pierce's room.

Hopefully, once she was with Pierce, she'd be able to focus on him and not think about the fact that Reuel was most likely in the other room gnashing his teeth.

She was so jittery, she dropped the gown she'd chosen twice before she managed to pull it over her head. All the sleeping gowns she'd bartered for since she'd arrived in Gallen were beautiful and alluring, to her mind at least, and all so sheer she felt the next thing to naked. She thought, perhaps, that something a little more conservative would make her feel less anxious, however, and chose the one that fell all the way to her ankles. Slipping her arms into the matching robe, she took several slow, deep breaths to calm her nerves and moved to the door.

She was more than a little disconcerted to discover the sitting room was empty and dark. Hesitant now, she stared at Pierce's closed door, wondering if she should go to him or not and finally shook her doubts off and crossed the room, tapping lightly on his door.

He opened it almost at once. He was bare foot, and bare chested, as if he'd been on the point of undressing for bed. Dalia swallowed nervously, wondering if she'd never actually seen him half naked before or she just hadn't noticed before how beautifully sculpted his body was. She felt her heart flutter nervously in her chest as his gaze slid slowly down her length and then up again. Without a word, he grasped her hand and pulled her into the room. They stood toe to toe, staring at one another for several moments. Finally, nerving herself, Dalia lifted a hand to his chest.

He jumped when she touched him. "Your hands are cold," he murmured, catching her hand between his and rubbing it.

Dalia bit her lip. Tugging her hand free, she dropped it to her side, gripping the folds of the gown. "I'm scar... nervous," she amended.

A slow smile curled his lips. Lifting a shaking hand, he slipped it along her shoulder, curling his fingers around her neck and tugging her toward him as he leaned down. "Never be afraid of me, Dally," he murmured, plucking almost playfully at her lips with his own.

Mesmerized, Dalia went perfectly still, holding her breath as warmth flowed through her veins. His ragged breath, sawing in and out of his mouth, brushed hers, mingled, flooded through her as she sucked in her breath sharply.

He lifted his head, slipped his hands along her shoulders and down to her waist. Pulling the belt free, he pushed the robe from her shoulders. It fell to the floor with the faintest whisper of sound. He looked the gown over, skated his hands over her breasts, cupping them, and finally hooked his fingers in the thin fabric at the neck of the gown and pushed it from her shoulders, as well. It slithered down her body, caught briefly on her distended nipples and then slipped free, settling around her hips.

He swallowed audibly as stared at her, finally lifting his hands and tracing the slope of her breasts with the lightest of touches, almost as if he was afraid to touch her, or feared she would vanish at his touch. "You're so beautiful, Dally," he whispered hoarsely.

Something warm and poignant traveled through her, not so much at his words but the way that he said them, that brought a hard knot of pain into her chest. To her horror, she felt tears well in her eyes. She blinked them rapidly, trying to dispel them, but he saw.

His face twisted. "We don't have to do this, Dally."

She shook her head, not trusting herself to speak, and surged toward him, wrapping her arms around his waist. He wrapped his arms around her without hesitation, rocking her slightly.

"It's all right, baby. Shhh."

"It's not all right," she managed.

He pulled a little away from her and scooped her into his arms. Carrying her to the bed, he sat down on the edge with her on his lap and caught her chin, forcing her to look at him. "No tears, Dally," he ordered, giving her a mock serious frown.

She sniffed, tried to smile and managed something more like a grimace.

He chuckled. "Was that supposed to be a smile?"

She chuckled, then sniffed again. "I don't suppose I could convince you to lay with me and cuddle?"

Grimacing, he released her and very carefully adjusted her gown, then took a deep, shuddering breath as if he were about to dive under water. "Anything for my Dally," he said. Turning, he dropped her onto the bed and then lay down beside her on his back. Tucking his hands behind his head, he stared up at the ceiling as she scooted close against his side and laid her cheek on his chest.

"I'm sorry," she murmured, stroking the little patch of dark blond hair that grew in the center of his chest.

He caught her fingers, holding her hand still. She could feel his heart beneath her fingertips, pounding hard and fast. He was holding his breath, struggling to regulate his rapid heartbeat. "I know. You always were too kindhearted for your own good, Dalia."

She thought it over and chuckled. "I'm a rogue hunter, Pierce. No one's ever accused me of being softhearted."

He threw her a feigned frown and then smote his head. "No wait! You're right! That was another female." Grinning, he rolled over onto his side, facing her. "You're the one that used to look so smug every time you beat the shit out of me in training."

"I never did!" Dalia said indignantly.

He laughed. "Ah ha! So you to admit you never beat me!"

The comment surprised a chuckle out of her. They'd only been paired off twice and she'd beaten him both times. "I was never smug about it. I knew I beat you because you couldn't get your mind off of my breasts." Smiling, she reached up and traced his laugh lines, wondering why it was that it had taken her so long to realize she loved him.

Shifting up on one arm, she pushed him onto his back once more and flicked the tip of her tongue back and forth across one male nipple a couple of times. Pierce sucked in his breath harshly, his fingers clenching in her hair. "Don't."

She lifted her head to look up at him.

He swallowed with an effort. "I don't have that much self-control, Dally."

Holding his gaze, she dipped her head once more and flicked her tongue across his other nipple.

He rolled, pushing her to her back, and lay half on top of her. There was no longer even a trace of amusement on his features. Dalia slipped her hands down to cup his buttocks and arched upward, grinding her mound against the hard ridge of flesh that lay across his belly. His face twisted with painful pleasure. "Dally!" he said breathlessly.

"I love you, Pierce," she murmured throatily, arching against him again. "Make love to me."

He stared down at her, obviously torn. "Don't ask me to stop again, Dally. I don't think I can," he ground out between clenched teeth.

"I don't want you to stop. I want to feel this inside of me," she murmured, slipping her hand between them and delving beneath his trousers to curl her fingers around his hardened flesh.

He groaned. Leaning down, he covered her mouth with his. The moment he did, she thrust her tongue into his mouth. He made a muffled sound from deep in his chest and sucked it, sending a dizzying tide of heat through her. Massaging his phallus, she coaxed his tongue into her mouth and sucked it.

Shuddering, he broke the kiss and leaned slightly away from her, studying her face. She opened her eyes with an effort and looked up at him.

Rolling off of her, he pushed his trousers down his hips and nudged them off, then turned to her and stripped her gown off. Tossing it aside, he ran a shaking hand over her almost reverently from her shoulder to her hip and then up again, cupping one breast. Dalia moaned in pleasure as he kneaded it in his hand and finally leaned down and covered the tip with his mouth, teasing the sensitive bud of tight flesh until she was breathless before moving to its mate and teasing that nipple with equal thoroughness.

Moving restlessly beneath him she caressed his arm, his shoulders, his back, every part of him that she could reach. Closing her eyes tightly, she felt the smoothness of his flesh beneath her palm and fingertips, the hard ridges of muscle. The muscles in her passage quivered, tensed, clenching and unclenching as if reaching for him. "Now, Pierce."

He lifted his head and looked at her, and then followed her gaze downward. Watching her hand as she parted her thighs wide and slipped it between her legs, parting the flesh for his gaze. He shifted down the bed. Sitting back on his heels, he caught her knees and pushed them upward, watching the movements of her fingers. After a moment, he grasped his sex and pushed the tip slowly inside of her, watching as her flesh parted for him, absorbed him. Leaning over her, he scooped an arm beneath her hips and pressed slowly inside her and then, just as slowly, withdrew.

Dalia leaned up to watch the joining of their flesh as well, felt her entire body tighten with desire as he continued to move slowly in and out, tantalizing her with the skate of his hard flesh inside of her. Groaning, she fell back, arched her head into the pillow. He released a harsh breath and drove deeply, grinding his hips against her, sending shards of exquisite pleasure through her as he rubbed against her clit. "Oh," Dalia moaned. "Like that, Pierce." She licked her lips, digging her fingers into his arms.

His arms began to shake with effort as he continued thrusting into her, pushing deeply and grinding his hips against her clit and then retreating. She caught his hips, urging him to move faster, to delve deeper as she hovered, suspended in a poignant torment of pleasure. A little cry escaped her as the first ripples of release shuddered through her. As if he'd been holding himself only for that, he settled his weight on top of her, opening his mouth over hers and absorbing her cries of delight as he pumped inside of her in short, hard thrusts.

Her release seemed to go on endlessly, the convulsions of her body so hard she felt blackness edge in on her. A thin sheen of sweat beaded his back when he shuddered once last time and fell still, lying heavily against her. She stroked his hair and back lovingly in appreciation, enjoying the feel of his weight.

Dragging in a final deep breath, he slid his arms around her and rolled over until she was lying on top of him. He stroked her back, her buttocks.

A shiver skated over her as her body cooled.

"Cold?"

"Only my back. My front's warmth," she murmured, smiling against his shoulder, feeling far too lazy to move.

Chuckling, he dumped her onto the bed and dragged the covers down, pushing and pulling at her until he had her arranged beneath the covers. When he was finally situated to his satisfaction, he gathered her against his side once more. "Better?"

"Mmmm," she said, almost purring.

He stroked her shoulder and back, slowly, mesmerizingly. "Dally?"

"Mmm?"

He was silent for several moments. "Why did you cry? Because it ... because it felt wrong?"

Sighing, she lifted her head to look at him, shaking her head slowly. "Because I spent most of the night last night, and all day worrying about what you'd said, wondering if I really did love you ... that way, or only as the dearest of friends. And then, when you kissed me, it felt so very, very right, that I knew you were wrong and I'd been worrying about nothing." She skated a hand down his stomach and ran it over his flaccid member. "I love you just exactly that way," she said, smiling in satisfaction as she felt his cock grow beneath her palm.

Chapter Twenty-Two

Despite her best efforts to tamp the afterglow of their night together in consideration of Reuel's feelings, she couldn't think that she'd been altogether successful, but then Pierce made no effort at all to hide his satisfaction. Every time she looked at him he was grinning, and every time he happened to catch her looking at him, a dull red blush would creep up his cheeks.

Reuel spent most of the day in the fields.

For months it seesawed like that, with first one and then the other wavering from fair mood to foul. After a time, however, they managed to rub along without so much tension when both Reuel and Pierce saw that she was true to her word and lavished attention upon them in equal parts.

On the first anniversary of their contract, they decided to celebrate in the city as they had celebrated the signing. Claire, a year old and often saying some really embarrassing things, sat in her chair like a little angel and managed to draw looks of approval as well as admiration, and even, Dalia thought, just a little envy from the couples sharing the restaurant with their own infants, who were as fussy as Claire had been the first time they'd come.

They were almost through with their dinner when she realized that tonight was her night to be with Reuel. She sent him a speculative glance, wondering what she might do to make it extra special for him since it was their anniversary.

Unfortunately, nothing really enterprising came to mind. Sighing in frustration, she glanced from Reuel to Pierce, who'd been unusually quiet. He was holding Claire in his arms, stroking her soft cheek with one finger, a faint smile on his lips as he studied her sleeping face.

A rush of love for both of them filled her, and then the realization that what she really wanted was to spend the night with both of her partners.

She wasn't entirely certain they were ready for that, but she decided, if the opportunity arose she would test the waters. It was Pierce's night to watch the baby, but she usually went right to bed now and hardly ever woke.

When they reached the plantation, Pierce led the way upstairs and took the baby to her room. Dalia trailed along behind him, casting a provocative glance over her shoulder at Reuel as she reached the upper landing and crossed the living area to her room.

She soaked in a hot bath, feeling the strain of the day slip away and the tension of anticipation take its place. Then she bathed in soap scented with flowers. When she'd finished, she dried herself and walked naked into the bedroom. The gown she'd chosen for Reuel lay across the bed where she'd left it. Lifting it by the shoulders, she examined the material with a sense of satisfaction. It looked as if it had been fashioned of gossamer. As she turned it, light gleamed off of it like sunlight on dew.

Separating the thin fabric, she pulled it over her head and went to study the effect in the mirror critically. The dark fabric lay like a shadow over her skin. Her nipples and the dark, curling hair between her thighs were as clearly visible as if only mist preserved her from nakedness. The neckline plunged halfway to her navel. The hem stopped at the tops of her thighs. Turning, she saw it fell short of covering the cheeks of her ass by a good two inches.

She felt aroused just wearing it.

She was fairly confident Reuel would find it--interesting.

He was lounging on the couch when she reached the living area, his arms propped behind his head, his legs sprawled on the top of the low table in front the couch. He glanced at her lazily where she stood in the doorway, watching him. His eyes glittered as his gaze slid up her as sensuously as a caress.

Pushing away from the door, she walked languidly toward him. He didn't move. He looked as if he was holding his breath. Turning when she reached him, she lifted one leg over his and straddled his lap. Sliding backwards slowly over the hard ridge beneath her buttocks, she lifted her feet and hooked her heels on the edge of the cushions, then leaned back against his chest. Lifting a hand to his cheek, she turned her face against his neck, breathing in his scent, nuzzling his ear with her nose, then tracing the swirls of his ear with the tip of her tongue.

He expelled a harsh breath and brought his arms down, dropping one on her flat belly. He slipped his other hand through the neck of her gown and strummed the edge of his thumb back and forth across her nipple until it stood erect, then pinched the erect nipple between his thumb and forefinger, plucking at it almost lazily.

Heat cascaded over Dalia's chest and belly like warm wine, intoxicating her. She sucked his earlobe between her lips, nipping at it gently with her teeth.

Shifting slightly, he lifted his hand from her belly and curled his fingers around her cheek and the back of her neck, plucking at her lips with his own teasingly before he opened his mouth over hers.

The sound of footfalls on thick carpet penetrated the haze of passion and both stiffened as they came near, then paused abruptly. Reuel's hand tightened on her when she would have pulled away, but she knew even without looking that Pierce had stumbled upon them.

She felt him watching.

Moist heat flooded her passage in a gush as her mind seemed to float free of her body and she found herself looking down upon the three of them; at Reuel, fondling her breast, kissing her, her legs splayed wantonly on either side of his thighs; at Pierce, mesmerized by the sight and unable to pull his gaze away.

She kissed Reuel back when he would have pulled away, slipping her tongue between his lips and exploring his mouth as he had hers. He groaned, arching his hips upward as he sucked at her tongue so that his rigid flesh dug into the cleft of her buttocks. Her short gown rode higher as he placed his feet on the floor. Slowly, he pushed her thighs apart, spreading them until the coolness of air licked along the heated, sensitive flesh of her sex and she felt the damp petals yielding gradually to the pressure of his knees against her thighs, opening like the deep pink petals of a dew laden flower.

When Reuel broke the kiss at last, he slipped his hand down her throat and beneath the neck of her gown to pluck at the nipple neglected of his attentions. Dalia moaned, arching her head against his shoulder even as she lifted heavy lids to gaze at Pierce across the room.

As if he sensed her watching him, he dragged his gaze upwards from her sex and met hers. She arched her body against the teasing torment of Reuel's hands, beckoning him closer. He swallowed as Reuel released one nipple and slipped that hand down her belly, raking a thick index finger along her cleft, smoothing the petals of flesh wide so that cool air blew across her body's opening.

Dalia gasped, squeezing her eyes closed as Reuel's touch sent a sharp knife of pleasure through her, making the muscles of her channel quake and clench with anticipation. When she opened her eyes again, she saw that Pierce had moved closer, his gaze riveted to the movements of Reuel's hand as he plucked and teased her clit, slipped his thick index finger inside of her, moving it slowly in and out before he traced her cleft again.

He shifted her on his lap, shoving his trousers down his hips far enough he could grasp his erection and free it. His cock landed, thick and heavy, against her cleft as he released his hold on it. He pressed his hand against it, rocking her hips so that his cock slid teasingly along her cleft. She moved with him for several moments. Finally, catching Pierce's gaze, she pushed Reuel's hand away and wrapped her fingers around his thick cock. Lifting up slightly, she pressed the rounded head inside of her. A rush of pleasure went through her. Bearing down with careful pressure, she worked his erection deeper, then lifted once more, feeling the flesh of her sex yield, and then cling to him.

Reuel groaned, and she heard Pierce swallow audibly, heard the rush of his breath. Spreading her thighs wider, she leaned forward, bracing her palms on Reuel's knees and bearing down with slow, deliberate pressure until she felt his cock stretching her to her limits. Catching her buttocks in his hands, Reuel arched upward even as he bore down on her, sinking more deeply still. A groan of pleasure scraped along her throat. She arched her head back, feeling her breasts sway with the movement, swinging free of the gaping neck of her gown.

When she managed to open her eyes again, she saw that Pierce was absently rubbing his cock, his gaze on her swaying breasts. She lifted up, allowing Reuel's cock to slide out of her until only the head remained inside, until Pierce could see where their bodies joined.

She licked her lips. "Let me see it," she said huskily.

Pierce's startled gaze moved to meet hers, but after only a brief hesitation, he pushed his trousers down his hips and kicked them off, freeing his cock, massaging it. Groaning at the heat that went through her, Dalia pressed down again, forcing Reuel's cock deeply inside of her. Again, he arched to meet her, bearing down on her buttocks harder than before. She squeezed her eyes shut, arching her head back as pleasure akin to pain tore through her.

She sensed that Pierce had moved close moments before she felt his mouth open over the tip of one undulating breast. He sucked her nipple hard, sending another harsh jolt of pleasure through her as she lifted her hips high and then pushed down again. She whimpered in pleasure, her mind black with it, her body feeling as if it was on fire as Reuel forced her into a faster rhythm, each time allowing his cock to slide almost completely from her body before driving it almost painfully deep.

And all the while, Pierce sucked first one nipple and then the other, teased them with his tongue, until she began to struggle to keep her climax at bay, striving to hold onto the pleasure just a little longer.

Just when she thought she couldn't hold back any longer, Pierce ceased his sweet torment of her nipples. With an effort, she opened her eyes.

He was kneeling in front of her, massaging his cock. She leaned forward as Reuel began pounding into her harder and harder, reaching for his own culmination. Flicking her tongue out, she dragged it slowly over the rounded tip of his cock, licking the sensitive head with slow deliberation. He groaned, gripping her shoulder, shifting slightly closer. She opened her mouth over him, sucking the head of his cock and then running her tongue around the sensitive ridge at its base.

A jolt of heat went through her. Pierce groaned, his fingers clenching in her hair.

Lifting her hands from Reuel's knees, she caught Pierce's hips, pulling him toward her as she opened her mouth wide to take his erection fully inside her mouth. He shuddered, began to move his cock in and out of her mouth, matching the jolting rhythm that Reuel set as he pumped his cock into her harder and faster, and so deeply each thrust sent another shaft of mind numbing, almost painful pleasure through her until she whimpered with the effort to contain it.

His fingers clenching and unclenching on her shoulder, Pierce shook as she held his erection tightly in her mouth, resisting his thrust and retreat, sucking on him as her body hovered on the verge of release. Abruptly, Dalia felt her belly clench, spasm with the first waves of culmination. She groaned, sucking Pierce's cock harder as it washed over her in increasingly hard waves. His cock jerked in her mouth as he reached his own crisis. Feeling his effort to withdraw, she dug her fingers into his buttocks, sucking him harder, refusing to release him as his crisis fed her own pleasure. He lost the battle, cried out hoarsely as his body convulsed in release and his hot seed spewed into her mouth. She sucked him greedily, gripping him until his body ceased to spasm in release.

With a growl of satisfaction, Reuel rammed deeply inside of her, bearing down on her hips as his orgasm spilled from him in convulsing waves.

Releasing her hold on Pierce at last, Dalia braced her shaking arms on Reuel's knees, panting for breath. Pierce sat back, bracing his fists on the table on either side of him, his head drooping forward on his shoulders as he, too, struggled to catch his breath. "I thought you were going to kill me," he muttered hoarsely.

Gathering herself, Dalia pushed back until she was leaning against Reuel's chest once more, caressing his cheek as she studied Pierce. "It was good for me, too," she said, stretching in satisfaction.

Pierce looked up at her a long moment and finally shook his head. Smiling faintly, he got up, snatched his trousers from the floor and departed.

Reuel grunted. "Did you enjoy yourself?" he asked, keeping his voice carefully neutral.

Dalia twisted around until she was seated across his lap. "You didn't?"

A shiver skated through him. He caressed her cheek, dropping a light kiss on her forehead and then her eyelids. "Immensely. But on my nights, I want you all to myself."

Chuckling, she looped her arms around his neck. "I'm all yours."

His eyes gleamed. Slipping one arm around her back, and one beneath her knees, he stood up and strode into his bedroom with her. "You're incorrigible," he muttered.

She laughed. "I'm not. I'm very, very good. And that was an anniversary present, for both of you, from me, with all my love."

Epilogue

Dalia felt like purring with satisfaction. There were a lot of reasons for it.

The first had been her first real dinner. She'd spent most of the day in the kitchen studying a computer screen to prepare the meal she'd planned. It was nothing short of amazing that it had been successful. She'd learned to use the strange cooking machines Reuel had in his house months ago, learned to use them adequately, not well.

On her cooking days, she managed to prepare a reasonably nutritious meal that was reasonably edible, but there was no getting around the fact that both Reuel and Pierce were much better at cooking than she was.

She had something special to announce tonight, however, and she'd decided that the best way to go about it was to feed them well, then fuck them well, and then, when they were completely mellowed and putty in her hands she would make her announcement.

They were surprised when they saw she'd set the table in the formal dining room downstairs, amazed at the beauty and variety of the dishes she set on the table. But they were absolutely stunned when they discovered that the food actually tasted good, too.

When she'd settled Claire for the night, she went into her room and prepared for phase two.

Reuel and Pierce were in the middle of a game of chess when she strolled from the room and sat down on the couch, too involved to begin with to notice her. Finally, Reuel had glanced toward her with a smile on his face that froze. Pierce, alerted by Reuel's expression, glanced at her and then did a double take.

She smiled at them, wagging her knees casually.

The two men exchanged a look, as if they were trying to figure out who the invitation was for. "Both," Dalia murmured, crooking her finger at them as she got up and headed back to her room.

They'd only engaged in a three way twice before and both times it had been, mostly, an accidental encounter. She'd never summoned them both and they glanced at each other uncomfortably for several moments before they both rose abruptly and followed Dalia into her room.

She was lying on the bed, propped up on one arm.

Pierce skimmed out of his clothing and joined her before Reuel had his boots off.

Grinding his teeth, Reuel finished undressing and moved to the other side of the bed, skating his hand down her back and cupping her buttocks. She rolled onto her back when Pierce broke the kiss and Reuel took the opportunity to fondle her breasts, teasing them with his fingers. Pierce watched as he leaned down to suckle one nipple and abruptly moved to the end of the bed. Catching Dalia's legs, he parted them and covered her mound with his mouth.

Dalia gasped, feeling her body rocket from desire to mindless passion within seconds as they teased her with equal finesse, unable to focus on any one point of stimulation as their mouths worked magic on her body and it climbed screamingly toward release.

Gasping, she squeezed her eyes closed and allowed her body to respond without restraint. Within moments, jolts of pleasure went through her as her body convulsed in release.

When she opened her eyes, she saw that both of them were studying her.

Weakly, she rolled onto her side and then got up on her knees. Pushing Reuel to his back, she caught his cock in her hand and ran her tongue around the head, sucked it, licked it again. He gripped the bed, groaning.

For several moments, Pierce merely sat back on his heels, watching. Finally, he moved around behind her and pushed her legs apart, pushing inside of her. She groaned, feeling her belly clench, feeling it burgeon with renewed need.

Moving slowly at first, and then more quickly as their desire built, they pleasured one another.

Her second climax hit her harder than the first, went on longer. She groaned as it washed over her, moving over Reuel greedily, until her urgency communicated itself to him and his body began to convulse with his own release. Pierce gripped her hips harder and raced to meet his crisis even as the last echoes of her climax began to fade.

Sated, exhausted, they collapsed on the bed together in a tangle of arms and legs.

Dalia rolled to her back, her head on Reuel's stomach, drowsing slightly as Reuel smoothed her hair. Pierce shifted and dropped his head on her stomach, caressing her hip and thigh.

Dalia sighed. The only thing she liked better than sex with Reuel, or Pierce, was sex with Reuel and Pierce. She thought about and amended it to sometimes.

"We're going to have a baby," she said.

Both Reuel and Pierce sat up abruptly, dumping her onto the bed.

"Whose?" they said almost in stereo.

Dalia chuckled and glanced at Reuel lovingly. He'd been undergoing experimental 'treatments' they hoped would make him capable of producing viable sperm. He'd never actually said anything after that one time when he'd admitted that he hadn't been capable of impregnating her, but she knew it tormented him to think he couldn't.

When she glanced at Pierce finally, she saw that he was trying not to look crestfallen. Sitting up, she put one arm around Pierce's neck, and one around Reuel's. Leaning close to Reuel, she kissed his cheek. "Yours." She turned to Pierce and kissed his lips. "And yours."

They looked at her blankly. "Mine or his?"

Sometimes they sounded like twins.

"Both," she clarified.

Reuel and Pierce exchanged a confused, and not very pleased, glance. "We both did it? Is that even possible?"

Dalia started laughing. "You ask me this when we started out as machines on an assembly line?"

They still looked more stunned than thrilled. Leaning back, she caught one of Reuel's hands and one of Pierce's and carefully placed them on her belly. "The boy is Reuel's. The girl is yours, Pierce."

The End

Printed in the United States
38094LVS00001BA/40

9 781586 087029